WITHOUT EXPIRATION

a personal anthology

WILLIAM R. HINCY

Book Design: Dario Ciriello
Cover Art: Kerry Ellis
Editing: Dario Ciriello, Marcia Meier

Library of Congress Control Number: 2019900260

ISBN 978-17327579-0-5 (print)
ISBN 978-17327579-1-2 (ebook)

First paperback edition: November 2019

Prior working versions of stories from *Without Expiration* were published as follows:

"Amen"—first published in *Passages North (2012)*

"Bermuda Triangle"—first published in *Oracle (2016)*

"Best if Used By"—first published in *Short Story America (2013)*

"Flying"—first published in *Ancient Paths (2005)*

"Left to Soak"—first published in *Ellipsis (2005)*

"Oceans"—first published in *The Rockford Review (2014)* and republished in *California's Emerging Writers (2018)*

"Teeth"—first published in *Avalon Literary Review (2016)*

"Years of the Dog"—first published in *Watershed (2017)*

Query by email to inquiries@whiskey-wingedlit.com.

Learn more at williamrhincy.com

CONTENTS

To dispelled magic, unfinished stories, missing middles, failed rebellions, and the speckled, gleeful light that dances upon them all

—WRH

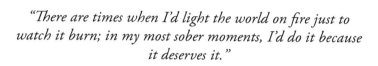

"There are times when I'd light the world on fire just to watch it burn; in my most sober moments, I'd do it because it deserves it."

BERMUDA TRIANGLE

"IT WOULD BE DARLING to be a poet. Yes, that's what strikes my fancy at the moment—I want to describe the bulb of a mother's belly when she first shows as the mound in the sand of a betrayed pirate."

"That's an unsettling image. Don't you poets write pretty things, like sonnets and ballads?"

"Rubbish, Charles. American education is so crass. Poets make interesting observations, not pretty ones."

"I see, but who would bury a betrayed pirate?"

She looked into his eyes, searchingly. "*I would*. I'd bury him right there on the Bermuda beach so he could still smell the sea."

"Have you been to Bermuda?"

"No, I've never been. But I saw a picture in an encyclopedia when I was a schoolgirl, and I can still remember how real the sensation of sand clinging to my feet felt. Bermuda is the child of a shipwreck, you know? Pilgrims on their way to the New World crashed there and didn't have any way off, so they started a colony."

"That's romantic, if an accident can ever be romantic. That's how all colonies should be started—with a shipwreck."

"Accidents are far more romantic than anything planned." She kissed his chest. "I don't think I'll ever forget the smell of your cologne. No matter how long it's been."

"I like the way your hair feels against my chest."

"This mop? It's so unmanageable and frizzy—I should do it for you more."

"You do it for me enough."

She nestled closer, wrapping her leg around his belly. "I've always believed that whole philosophy of The One was rubbish—complete hogwash. But as far as chests go, yours is definitely *The One*."

"Only your accent could make the word *hogwash* sound poetic."

"It feels good to hear someone responding to my voice again. For months now Terrance has only been home long enough to sleep. It's impossible for a wife to compete when her husband's mistress is himself."

"The best thing you can do if you want to ignore someone is marry them."

"Oh, he was ignoring me long before we were married."

"He's a scoundrel. I could never marry you."

"We're all scoundrels, darling. He just knows how to fulfill himself with a completeness I never could. Why should I want to leave the needs of someone I love unfulfilled?"

"You don't love him."

"Why? Because I *can* stay away from him? Because I don't cry or bleed for him? Maybe that is love."

"Don't talk about him. I can't bear it."

"So interesting the things we can and can't bear. There never seems to be any sense to it, yet, somehow, it all makes perfect sense."

"My American education couldn't understand that."

"I can see the Irish in your face when you're witty—your nostrils redden and flare." With a finger, she flicked the tip of his nose. "Tell me, do you talk to your wife this way?"

"Yes."

"Does she lay her head on your chest?"

"Yes."

"As she should. It's a perfectly brilliant chest for laying your head upon. Terrance's has always been too boney for my taste."

"Please, I just want to forget about him."

"You men. Such weak bellies and fragile egos. I don't mind thinking of you and your wife at all. In fact, I'm fascinated by it. The thought of you lying together so intimately, yet you with so many shadows. So much of you I know that she doesn't. I like being the mistress in that way. The wife is such a dreary, predictable role."

"Amelia, there's nothing predictable about you—no, no, don't move. I was just adjusting my arm. Can you hear that? I think it's starting to rain."

She paced her fingers up his forearm. "I wonder what our baby would look like?"

"Frizzy hair and soft chest, I'd bet."

She smiled. "You always did make me laugh. *Do*—you do make me laugh."

He tightened his grip around her. "Amelia, we *could*—you know?"

"Let's not talk about those things. Not now."

"Is there anything I can do?"

"Yes. Be the Bible, be Shakespeare—tell me everything and nothing at all."

"To be or not to be, thou shalt not!"

"*Ha!* I pity the children born here."

With his free hand, he stroked her from shoulder to elbow. "I miss the way your skin feels pressed against mine."

"My skin? It's so dry. I really should moisturize more often." She examined her left hand against the backdrop of his chest. "Do you think you'll ever tell her about us?"

"I'd lose everything if I did."

"You'd be nothing without her, and *I'd* still want you. Your wife cares only about her marriage, nothing about you."

"I'm not sure I'd love you if I were nothing."

"Rubbish. It's only then that you could love me at all." She traced his ribcage with her cheek. "I wonder what it would feel like to have a little foot kick me in the ribs."

"I can kick you if you want to find out."

"Not funny, Charles."

"I'm kidding. I could never kick you with this bum knee."

"How did you do it with the other women? How did you remain so impassive when they came crying to you? When their hearts were slit for you?"

He examined the ceiling, drawing daisies with his finger on her shoulder. "I explained that it was a stage of grief, and once they were past the deal-making phase they'd be able to move on. And I never grieved."

"You know I never expected this to happen. I took my wedding vows quite seriously when I was making them. But a man with a chest like Terrance's can give you such a knot in the neck."

"Don't talk of him. I like to imagine it's just you and me when we're together. Just our skin and heartbeats."

"But it's not just you and me and *our* heartbeats."

"I know. That's what scares me."

"I think I will be a poet." She laid her hand on her belly. "I do like the image of the soft white lump of a pirate buried in a shallow grave. I think I'll always remember it, even if I do decide I want to forget."

"We could, Amelia—*I would?*"

"Hush, my darling nothing. It's only a stage of grief."

BEST IF USED BY

No one is ever there when you need help putting things away. As any mother can attest, this is especially true for the groceries. I've spent my adult life bringing in and putting the groceries away by myself. On the rare occasions when John would help, he would hang all of the grocery bags on his wrists and side-step into the house with his arms outstretched like a homeless messiah carrying all of his belongings in bags for lack of a buggy. I used to call him lazy for not wanting to walk out to the car multiple times, but now as I bring the groceries in by myself, I do the same. I can't carry as much as him, though, and the handles of the plastic bags dig into my bone and leave long canals in the skin across my wrists. As I step into the kitchen, I can't take the searing pain in my right wrist from a bag pregnant with a gallon of milk, so I lay all of the bags on the linoleum floor. Freeing myself from these colorful torture devices, I rub my wrists one at a time, trying to circulate the blood. I wish it were John's wrists that were in pain, but men are as useful as unset alarm clocks, and the pain is mine alone.

"Everything okay?" John asks, and the scent of fajitas frying on the stove—the garlic, the onions, the jalapeño, the ghost peppers he cultivated in the garden out back—suddenly itch deep inside my nose.

"Shut up," I say, even though I know he's not there. And his whiny voice and the tingle of the spicy peppers disappear in the mirror of the moment.

I crouch down and begin to forage through the bags, looking for the items that need to be refrigerated. Pulling out the TV dinners, I cross to the refrigerator and stuff them neatly into the freezer. The kitchen is so small it could never comfortably fit two people at the same time, so it only takes me a step to return to the bags and fetch more perishable items. The milk, the eggs, the butter—into the refrigerator. The chocolate ice cream—to the silverware drawer, where I pull out a spoon, lean over the sink, and greedily devour a few scoops of melting ice cream. There's a window over the sink, but all you can see from it is the window to the kitchen of the apartment across the way. The mother is washing dishes, her wedding ring, the diamond no bigger than a freckle, dangling from a chain on her neck. She is heavy-set, and the sight of her full face laboring over the sink makes me squeamish. I slip one more spoonful of ice cream into my mouth and put the carton away.

There's nothing left that needs to be put in the refrigerator, so I pick up the last couple of bags and place them on the counter. I open the top cupboards; everything inside is positioned in perfect order. In fact, everything in the kitchen is exactly the way I want it, and there isn't anything I like about it. I dig into a grocery bag and slide a box of saltine crackers into place next to a box of Holden's fruit snacks. There is a pastel red dinosaur on the front of the fruit snack box—a brachiosaurus, I think—with a goofy grin and bright eyes, and I happen to glimpse the Best If Used By date stamped on the dinosaur's neck in block letters: December 2009—four years ago.

"I can't believe you kept those," John says again.

"Shut up," I say.

I remember Holden's face—his high chubby cheeks scrunched, and his eyes bulging beneath eyebrows arched in bottomless pyramids—as he toddled around the house holding a plastic dinosaur out with both hands and growling: "Die-no-soar—*roar*!" He was two years old, so tall for his age he looked like he was five, and "dinosaur" was among his first fifty words. Our house had a built-in oak bar in the study that he would hide in, stuffing himself in next to the bottles of scotch and brandy, and shaking his head defiantly any time we tried to pry him out. He would refuse to come out until I would finally offer him a pouch of fruit snacks. John always warned me against spoiling the boy, but I had always retorted, "Children aren't onions—they don't spoil." And even though there is no study or bar or scotch in my apartment, I can still picture Holden sitting there tucked behind his chubby, block legs, waiting for me to offer him a fruit snack.

I set a box of Raisin Bran next to the Lucky Charms, and I can hear Holden's distant giggling interrupted by a plaintive grunt. They were his favorite—he would drag me over to the pantry by a finger to make him a bowl and would never believe me if there wasn't any left. Pulling the box of Lucky Charms from the shelf, I check the expiration date and press the box to my breast. January 2010. The date says it has been expired for three years. But there are those things with no expiration. Even if one day the faculty for memory dissolves blissfully into fits of dementia, the effects of that memory will remain as cutting and aromatic as the day they were made. So no, Holden's favorite cereal is not expired—and his fruit snacks are still as good now as they were on the date printed on the package.

"We're all parented by the past, so it's perverse when you marry it," John had said shortly before filing for divorce. He wanted me to put everything behind me, to move on, but nothing is ever behind you when you're surrounded by mirrors. I reach into the plastic bag, remove the last item, a jar of spaghetti sauce—Holden had always hated spaghetti—and set it on the shelf next to the old fruit snacks, the expired Lucky Charms, the unperishable pain.

LEFT TO SOAK

HELEN KNEW when she got home there would be, among other things, dishes to do. In forty-six years of marriage, Hank had never washed a single dish. And Helen could do the math, oh yes, she could, though he would have you believe otherwise. She could calculate—with just a piece of paper and a pencil, even while lying in a hospital bed—that at a rounded-off estimate of twenty dishes a day (not to mention silverware—that was another story), every day, 365 days a year, for forty-six years (not including the nuisance of leap years), she'd done a whopping... 335,800 pots, pans, plates, bowls, etcetera, to his—*zero*. She imagined if you tallied up the score to all of their Rummy games he wouldn't make out much better. To counter this, he would undoubtedly cackle on about the score in the earnings department, of which he was the clear victor—unless he was squared off against another *average* man, in which case he would be pummeled.

Hank had provided for them well enough, and Helen would never soil his pride by saying otherwise. They had a quaint home, Hue, their only child, had never wanted for food or warmth, and Helen was never forced to look like one of the train-hopping bums she read about in the magazines and saw some of the other ladies in town dressing like. But Hank was an impatient dreamer and had thus seen nothing but the ends, choosing to ignore and chastise the means with his unique blend of wit and vulgarity. Had Hank been paid for his wit, they unquestionably would have been living in a mansion, sipping on whatever drink was trendy at the time while patronizing the help. But he never earned a dime for his wit, so instead, they lived off of the small salaries he earned from working hard, but never long, at one place.

"If you were meant to stay with one job all your life they'd call it the mob," Hank would say.

Hank had a flair for expression that at times was annoying, but most of the time was at the very least amusing. Some of his notorious sayings were: "Mama Earth only spreads her legs for the man with the accent," and, "Only the discontent can invent," and, Helen's favorite, "It's hard to become rich when you're robbin' the bank of your own money." And every night when they went to bed after she'd finished with what had somehow become *her* duty—the dishes—he would say, dumbly, with dry hands:

"Dream of me, darlin'."

Helen's roommate in the bed next to her, Judy, thought that Hank's goodnight saying was sweet. In fact, whenever Hank was out of the room—which wasn't nearly often enough—she'd croon on and on about Hank-this and Hank-that. Every time she said Hank's name aloud it startled Helen; for her, his name had been scrubbed off long ago. Immediately after marriage, his name was lengthened to "Hank-honey." From here it was reduced to "Honey," and then "Hun." After Hue was born, he became "Dada," "Daddy," "Dad," "The Old Man," and after Hue married and had little Charles, Hank's name soaked away into "Grandpap," "Grandpa," "Granddaddy," and "Papa," all of which made Helen uncomfortable because they made her feel old by association.

Hank did have his virtues, though with time they had begun to wrinkle worse than his face. He was smart, often to the point of annoyance: Sometimes he spoke with the tone of Father Time beckoning the seasons. But his skill with observation and judgment came in handy around voting time when she had to wade through the smiles and insistent political jabs to find a fork of truth. The way Hank put it was: "Lawyers become politicians when they're too crooked to obey laws anymore, so they have to make them. The only bigger crook is an auto mechanic. If mechanics ever become politicians the only thing that will ever get fixed in this country is their pocketbooks." And he should know: He'd done a stint as a mechanic back in the sixties for a few years. He quit abruptly after his boss, an old friend from his service days, had called him a lazy asshole after he'd taken a busy day off to spend with Helen since it was her fortieth birthday. Certainly, that was a virtue—probably his best: He'd give anything up for her, even if it were just to spend the day together.

"Dream of me, darlin'."

But none of that changed the fact that the lazy old man had never picked up a single dish and *scrubbed* it. Once, he'd set his cereal bowl in the sink, flipped the faucet on and then—just as quickly—flipped it off. Then he waltzed out of the house with his raggedy brown fishing hat pulled down over his eyelashes, concealing the bald, wrinkled arch of his head, to go fishing with the same man who had called him a lazy asshole fifteen years before. Hank would forgive the devil for causing him to smoke if it was the Christian thing to do. He *was* a fisherman of some merit; he had even won two tournaments in his prime. He'd appeared in the local newspaper, the *Granite Creek Intruder*, after he won the Broken Toe County fishing tournament of 1967. So it wasn't that Hank didn't like getting wet, it was just that dishwater repelled him in the same manner that a sickly buck repels a doe.

Every year, Hank, as if a clock losing seconds, became lazier. And every year Helen became more and more angered by the growing certainty that The Old Man would never wash a solitary dish. Sometimes she'd be splashed by a frigid icing of animosity, and, as was her custom, she would sit quietly, coolly, throughout the evening, without saying a single word if possible, until she would lay down on *her* side of the bed, curl into a neat ball, and go to sleep without kissing, touching or even looking at Hank. He referred to this as "one of Grandma's moods," as if it was bad gas caused by barbecue sauce. She didn't think it was that difficult to figure out the cause of her moodiness, but instead of even trying, Hank would chalk it up to some sort of feminine defect.

"Dream of me, darlin'."

It was hard to stay mad at him for long, though, because even now, after forty-six years of marriage, he still held her hand tightly and walked *right* beside her whenever they went anywhere. Sometimes when her knees were ailing, and the pain swelled and throbbed beneath the cruel layers of years, Hank would wheel her around in her wheelchair—proudly, as if it were ordained that her feet not touch common ground. She hated using the wheelchair, hated, even more, to be seen in public with it, but Hank could not be trusted to do the shopping, not even with a list. Helen remembered the way his youthful lips felt like warm honey; she could remember them so vividly that sometimes she would be washed away by fantasies of the way he had once touched her. And he had never denied her his touch, no matter how tired or sick he was, until recently. It was his heart: It sputtered from time to time and quite frankly scared the hell out of Helen. But the years had been especially vindictive through Hank's lips, as they now felt like dry slivers of jerky, and occasionally they would prick her skin. He wouldn't apologize when this happened; he would just remark, coolly:

"You really have gone allergic to me."

Helen tried not to be bitter with Hank, Hank-honey, Dada, The Old Man, but it was difficult when she'd yearn for the cool sterility of the museums, the musty smell of the playhouses, the sensory chaos of the malls—the moving, living history of the city. *Home*. To Helen, the city had been home, but Hank had some whimsical notion that home had to be found like an Easter egg or a vein of gold. He preached about finding "someplace to call home." To raise kids. To stake a claim to. To live off the fat of the land, maybe get rich off that fat, and then buy more of it to litter with horses and cows so they could feed off the same fat while Helen died slowly, *her* hands drowning in tediousness, searching through the suds of mediocrity and the dingy water of strife for an aesthetic moment or anything that wasn't *from the earth*. But Hank had dreams of the simple: of earth, of minerals, of *silver*. Which led to the mountains of Colorado, to rapt ignorance, to the echoes of "Goddamnit" reverberating through the canyons, to the endless sight of women with teary faces, of teenagers trekking off with their fathers into the damned mines: to godforsaken Granite Creek, Colorado. To Hank, it had glistened with opportunity. To him, it had seemed perfect, ideal, *dreamy*. To Helen, it was a broken toe, and it stranded her in a life of mundanity, forcing her to hobble among the hopeful and subsequently hopeless. But mostly it forced her to stand in front of a sink perpetually swimming with dirty dishes, her once gentle hands dissolving to calluses as they feverishly, day after endless day, scrubbed them clean—for forty-six years, with absolutely no help.

Some of the other ladies on the block had dishwashing machines. The advertisements called them the modern woman's most valuable accessory. And Helen had read—and heard from her younger sister who owned one and liked to rub that fact in—that all the women in the city *and* suburbs had one, and all the new homes were being built with them. But Granite Creek wasn't a city or suburb; it was a garbage disposal of ignorance flooded with poverty that would never be washed away. And Helen knew without asking that Hank would never consent to a dishwasher as long as she had two working hands. Besides, it had become a point of pride with Helen, as she had done the dishes by hand for this many years without aid, and she'd be damned if she would accept any now.

Helen had watched Hank venture into the mines on four occasions. Each stint was shorter than the last, as they both knew that he was no miner. Thankfully, Hue had been Helen's boy, and as such he had left immediately following high school for Boulder, and the college therein. Helen realized he was indeed her boy when he was only two years old—he learned his alphabet and sang its infamous song all day long—and therefore she had been careful not to lie with Hank again when she was fertile. It had worked, and she was spared the agony of watching one of her sons—she refused to think of what would have happened had she had a daughter—get lost in the mines or bounce from job to job as his wife slaved in the kitchen, doing *his* dishes, while his hands remained flat and dry on his seat in the living room.

Not that it was only the dishes that Papa had never helped with. He had also never washed or hung a stitch of clothing—though Helen would've never let him because he no doubt would've done *something* wrong—nor had he vacuumed the floor or dusted. But dusting didn't prune her hands, nor did running the sweeper, and neither of those chores was as insidious or as unrelenting as the damned dishes.

Two years before, the Granite Creek Intruder had done a special on their forty-fourth wedding anniversary, touting them as the city's longest-running marriage. The reporter had asked them questions separately. Then he asked them questions together. Hank had been downright proud of this occurrence. He had, in fact, framed the article and displayed it, much to Helen's dismay, above the living room fireplace. He boasted, quite frequently at the time, that every year from now on the paper would have to do another article on them because they were only getting older.

Helen hated the article. All it did was remind her of the dryness of his hands. The entire time the reporter spoke, all she could think was: *Hank and Helen: the World's Oldest Couple. Hank: the world's oldest dreamer. Helen: the world's oldest hands.* And she had scorned Hank for his boisterousness, and for his ignorance of her, and for displaying the article like a trophy when it was more like a traffic ticket. And she'd spent many nights sullen, quiet, curled up neatly on her side of the bed. Of this, Hank had just remarked: "The oldest couple—Grandma's oldest *mood.*"

She did not snap out of her mood until Hank, without provocation, decided to take her to see Hue and the family in Colorado Springs. Perhaps he did it as a peace offering—Helen's intuition told her this was so—but either way, it wiped off the residue left from the interview and allowed her to concentrate on happier things. She loved to visit Hue and the family, but Colorado Springs was two hours and three interstate highways away, an intimidating journey to Helen, who didn't enjoy driving the ten minutes to the market.

Hank didn't like the trip to Colorado Springs, either. It was his belief that traveling should be left to the young. But he was willing to make the drive, though not nearly as often as Helen would have liked. She did get to see baby Charles quite often, though, because Hue would bring him up to Granite Creek seemingly on a whim. But that still left her in Granite Creek—the museum of the wretched—with her hands always just inches away from the sink.

Hank had held her hand all night, all three nights she was held up at the Lockly hospital. He went home for only a couple of hours each day to shave, shower and take a nap, and Helen knew he couldn't be getting *any* of the housework done. The doctor told her to conserve her energy because her lungs hadn't yet regained their strength, so she tried her best *not* to think about the dishes. So she said nothing to Hank about the dishes, or about anything at all. She just lay in bed, her mind soaking in the inevitabilities of life, trying not to be sad, discouraged or angered. Instead, she tried to scrub away the realization that the love—the man—she had desired when she was young had only proven to sully the life her aging self would have liked to have been able to remember.

"Dream of me, darlin'."

"Marry me, darling." He'd said as they waited in line at the playhouse almost half a century ago.

Yes—she said yes without thought, without even being asked a question. She had loved him; she had wanted him; but she had not really known him. She didn't know that the depths of his love would keep him by her side, Hank-honey, The Old Man, without sleep, holding her hand, sobbing from time to time when he thought she was asleep when she was just ignoring him, praying to a God who had previously only been the man of the hour at a social gathering on Sundays, pressing her hand against his soft face but not kissing it out of fear his lips would prick her skin, asking the doctor when could his wife go home, but, more importantly, when would it be safe for her to go home. She hadn't known he could love her so much as to have to be forced to leave her side when the terror of losing her caused his heart to gurgle with the bubbling of a heart attack. But she also didn't know that this same man could be capable of the indifference necessary to strand his wife upon an ocean of dishes for forty-six years, without even once attempting to rescue her.

"It's time to go home."

To the house. To the *old* house. To the constant repetitive chores. To the ignorance. To the mines of lost dreams. To the perpetually grammatically incorrect newspaper. To Granite Creek, Colorado. To Hank, Hank-honey, Hun, Grandpa, Papa, The Old Man. To her companions—the dirty dishes.

"It'll be good to be home," Hank said as he and a male nurse helped her out of the hospital's wheelchair into their primer-gray Datsun.

Immediately upon taking her seat inside, she was greeted with the rank smell of Hank's sweat. Hank scurried around the back of the car with rigid, small movements, the waddle characteristic of old men in a hurry. Once inside, he turned the key and said, "Hue said he'd be up this weekend to see you."

She didn't respond.

They pulled onto the road. "Did you dream of me, darlin'?"

They drove on, moving slowly through the city streets as if sightseers on a leisurely drive. Helen looked out the window with pursed lips.

"Hue's sorry he didn't come up, but the baby had a bug, and he didn't want to leave him... The woman next to you—Judy something—she was nice, huh?"

Shooting a worried glance at her, Hank asked, "Not up to talking yet?"

"I bought some of that ChapStick, stuff," he said a few moments later.

Then, after another all-too-short pause: "Did you sleep well?"

Helen looked out the passenger window. Spanning into the distance, tall yellow grasses swayed, each strand rooted in position, stretching out to feel the sensation of movement and the sweet piercing sensation of approaching the moment it will snap.

"Goddamnit get the hell out of the fast lane, slow-ass!" Hank shouted.

Helen didn't bother to look away from the grasses.

"Some weather we're having, huh? Clear as June and we ain't halfway through winter, yet." Hank fidgeted with the radio dials, the air conditioner, the windows. "I think I'll change the oil tomorrow," said Hank, adjusting the seat that had been positioned exactly right for him for the past twelve years.

The grasses turned to houses, tract homes that flipped past like animation caught in a loop, portraying movement and utter stagnation all at once.

"We're here."

Hank hurried to open Helen's door and helped her out of the car and into the house. Inside was much as she'd left it. The emerald carpet was sporadically dotted with stars of lint, and the W's and V's that marked a freshly vacuumed carpet had dissolved into flattened squares. The stale odor of The Old Man's cannabis smoke clung to the air, musty and naturally sweet, somewhat pleasant in its earthiness after the sterility of the hospital. With one arm around her waist and the other holding her hand, Hank led Helen to the couch. The couch was heavily crossed with faded lime green and dark brown stitching, and the fabric was beginning to separate, revealing the piss-yellow cushions beneath. Helen couldn't stand to look at it, but the living room was inundated with the design, as the loveseat and Hank's big seat shared the revolting pattern and colors.

"Why don't ya sit down, darlin'?"

She didn't want to sit down.

"It'll be good for ya."

She wanted to see the state of the kitchen.

"Would ya rather go lay down?"

He wouldn't let go of her.

"I made the bed."

She didn't need his damn help just to stand.

"Are you hungry?"

She needed help with the dishes!

"Take me to the kitchen, Hank."

"Darlin', I'll get whatever ya —"

"Then let go of me, and I'll do it myself," she said.

"Sit down, dar—"

"Let go of me, you maddening old fool!"

"Helen, darlin'… All right."

She shuffled to the kitchen. Hank walked closely behind her, ready to catch her if her strength failed her. But it wouldn't. She was strong and determined, and if only to spite his *help,* she would not falter. She refused to give him that pleasure.

From the entranceway to the kitchen, she could see the mountains of dishes glistening in the afternoon sun like fool's gold. There were more than she remembered: *he'd* dirtied more. She trudged over to them with the inexhaustible will of a recaptured slave being taken back to the fields after a brief escape. She pushed the faucet handle up. Water squealed out and splashed off the dishes and onto her face. Reeking of mold, the sink looked like it had vomited all the contents of the garbage disposal. She grabbed the first dish. It felt cold and awkward in her hands, the way the silver must have felt to the first godforsaken prospectors of Granite Creek. Hank stood behind her, staring, silent. She realized that her bristle pad was buried somewhere beneath the dishes.

"Hank."

"Yes, darlin'?"

"Could you reach into the soap powder cupboard and get me a new bristle pad?"

"Of course. Which cupboard is that?"

"The one above the stove—you *do* know what the stove is, don't you?"

"Helen—"

"Get the bristle pad now, Hank."

"All right."

He reached into the cupboard, fumbled through the bottles of soap, and finally forked out the package of bristle pads. Bringing the entire bag to Helen, Hank looked like an old man forced into hard labor. He handed the bag to Helen, and then stood there with wide, dumb eyes.

"Darlin', you don't need to do this right now. You go sit down. The doctor—"

"The doctor's not here, *Grandpa*. Now leave me be."

Then she began her duty, mechanically, hands

scrunched into dried roses, heart like a cricket in a box. The water began to steam into her face, burning her eyes, but not her hands, her numb, homemaker hands. She moved all of the dishes from the basin on her left into the one on the right, and then onto the counter as needed. She filled up the empty sink with water and dish soap, and then began to fill it with the older dishes tumored by rotting food, her hands working faster and faster, moving in and out of the piles of slavery with the knowledge and purpose of a chipmunk retrieving nuts for its young. Her oppression renewed, she began to scrub the first dish: maddeningly, up and down, back and forth, swirling around and around, her hands pistons of routine, of labor. Then, reconciled to this bitter circumstance, she looked out the window that unquestionably is over every woman's cell, and looked upon a land that had been Hank's dream and her cage. A bird of some description took flight and soared out of her sullen view into the streaking rays and shimmering radiance of the sun. She felt like curling into her neat ball right there, in front of the sink, and going to sleep. Instead, she pivoted to her left to put the plate she had finished washing into the dish drainer.

But her path to the dish drainer was blocked by Hank. He was standing next to her with his hands immersed in the water in the left basin. Standing there—*scrubbing*—with determined, albeit futile, effort, the dishes she had left to soak, Hank once again glowed with the dashing stubbornness that had attracted her to him in their youth. With the steam billowing into his beautiful hazel eyes that had never aged a single day, he scrubbed the dishes with unflinching resolve, even though it was obvious that the water was burning his hands.

"Those need to soak a bit."

"It's okay—"

"No—"

"I've got them. An old man can make himself useful from time to time."

"Okay, Hank." She looked out the window and then said, properly, without looking at him, "Thank you."

And there they stood, side by side, *both* their hands wet, scrubbing the dishes as the world grew gray with dusk around them.

FRIENDLY STRANGER

DAMNIT!—my sole goal in life is to avoid waiting at a red light for more than one rotation, and, you guessed it, I've now been stuck for three infuriating cycles. It's the same maddening pattern over and over. Green left turn arrow, yellow, red. A few cars zip through, screeching tires, horns and curses blaring after them. Green. Wait for the cars still turning in front of you. Yellow. Speed through the intersection and come to a complete stop on the other side. Red. Step on the accelerator only to get stuck in the middle of the intersection, repeat horns, curses, and fingers. When I was a kid, I used to have to lie to my dad when he asked if I'd said my prayers. But if he were around now, I could answer him honestly because I'm praying for salvation from another afternoon Carmageddon.

Why am I here? Because some asshole, *Mr. Big Hurry Blue Infiniti*—with obnoxious "My Child Gets Better Grades than Yours" bumper sticker—cut me off so he could get into the left turn lane. To make a point, I smacked my horn and swerved into the lane he had vacated. Sure enough, Mr. Big Hurry made it through the light while I got stuck at it, so I guess the only point I made was that I'm a vengeful idiot.

Finally, I get past the light. *Immediately*, an eighteen-wheeler makes a right, pulling out in front of Old

Lady Mercury, Midlife Crisis Corvette, and me. Old Lady Mercury pulls to the side of the road and looks down at her lap, apparently checking to see if she has peed herself. Midlife Crisis begins to swerve back and forth in the lane and into oncoming traffic, jousting for an opportunity to speed past the truck. A block later Midlife makes a right turn into a residential neighborhood. A *slow* right, almost coming to a complete stop in the street before accelerating through the turn.

After jolting over six potholes, a traffic cone and what looks like it used to be a raccoon, I'm now on Angeles Crest Highway, a mostly one-lane thoroughfare leading from the Pasadena area through the San Gabriel Mountains to my home in the high desert. Still stuck behind the ginormous caterpillar with the "How's My Driving?" mud flaps, I pop in my AC/DC CD once the radio turns to static. After only a quarter mile—sweet Mother Carpool Lane—the eighteen-wheeler drifts over to the shoulder. I speed past, flashing a thankful palm at the trucker as I do. Without the sight of a slow-moving car—or *any* car—in front of me, I step on the gas and begin to sing along with AC/DC's "Highway to Hell."

Swerving, my tires screeching like pinched babies, I come around a bend that jolts into a quarter mile straightaway. Haphazardly tucked next to the mountain, its rear end jutting halfway out into the road, is the blue Infiniti belonging to none other than the maniac who had cut me off! As I approach, I can see Big Hurry standing in front of the Infiniti with his hands on his hips, shaking a weary head at the gaping mouth of the open hood. And he's *just standing* there in his green corduroy pants and *"I'm with Stupid→"* T-shirt like he's just given the hood a stern lecture and he's waiting for it to apologize for what it has done. Thanking Karma for this gift, I ready my finger. Load torpedo bay three. Fix on target…

Damn it! As I'm speeding toward him at seventy miles per hour, the wicked whim of Fate rears her sappy mane: somehow, despite the impossible odds, I manage to spot one solitary tear shining gold in the sunlight as it slides down Big Hurry's face. And for some ungodly reason—perhaps divined by all the wishy-washy romantic comedies my ex-girlfriend used to con me into watching—I pity this guy—*Mr. Big Hurry!* How em-*pathetic* I am.

With horror, I feel my car slowing as I stop to offer assistance to every jerk who has ever cut me off, rode my ass, refused to let me merge, went the speed limit in the fast lane, slowed down at a yellow light, and hesitated to accelerate at a green light. Suzy, my ex, is probably beaming right now—hell, if she knew that I was pulling over to help this selfish prick she might even come home.

As I pull to a stop—a neat, orderly maneuver, hardly kicking up any dirt or rocks, as close to the hip of the mountain as possible, only *25* percent of *my* car in the road—I curse myself for this sudden bout of conscience. Opening my door, I hear Big Hurry squeak:

"I don't have any money."

What? Does this guy think that I don't have a job, a life, that I'm some poor wretch in such desperate need that I'm going to pull over and rob a guy wearing an *"I'm With Stupid* → "T-shirt? I get out with my hands up like a criminal after a high-speed chase. "It's okay. I just thought maybe I could help you out. I—I used to be a mechanic."

I was never a mechanic, but if I am to do this show of goodwill that I feel compelled to do, then I have to put Big Hurry at ease.

"Oh—*great!* Oh, what a lifesaver." Suddenly enthusiastic, he bounds up to me as if he's approaching an old friend getting off a plane. "You're—wow—a *swell* guy.

I'm in such a hurry. Usually, I'm a cautious driver. I check—*literally*—the air in my tires *and* the oil level before I start the car. But I forgot to today. Dear God, I was in such a hurry that I cut someone off. I have to admit it was a kind of a thrill, but I feel terrible about it now.... My daughter, it's her first soccer game... I promised.... It's probably the oil, right?"

It's probably the oil? My God, man, take a class or something. Maybe *Common Sense 101.* There should be a mandatory test to keep cars out of the hands of idiots. Oh no. Oh, God. Tears are amassing their forces on the bottoms of his eyes, preparing to strike with the sympathy and shame that blitzes you whenever you see a grown man cry. Quickly I launch a counter-attack: "Oh, well, I know how that is. Daughters and all—*soccer.* We'll see what we can do. Get you back on the road—soccer game number one here we come!"

What a complete pansy I've become. I know how that is—*daughters and all?* Soccer game number one? Soccer is sickening. Me—sterile.

Big Hurry says, "My name's Stacy. I'm a secretary for the First Baptist Church of Glendale."

Why does every Baptist church claim to be the first? I wonder as I bend down under the hood. *Do they get loyalty points or their rents frozen in heaven?* As I fiddle with the engine, checking a couple of connections to make sure they are secure, I realize I don't have any idea what I should be doing. What is it precisely that car guys do under the hood? Is this *all* I should be doing? I have no idea what a broken carburetor would *look* like. I have a healthy understanding of how a car works and can usually diagnose what the problem is—but not by sight. "What happened?" I ask, emerging from beneath the hood. "How'd she quit on you?"

"She? Oh, no. This is my wife's car. *She's* a *he*."

"Oh—sorry. How did *he* die?"

"Oh, dear, I hope he's not dead. My wife would kick my *butt!* Excuse my language, but oh, jeez, am I in such trouble. My name's Stacy, by the way. I'm a secretary."

I think about my dad, who had been a minister up until the day he died, and suddenly feel a wash of pity for him for having to work with people like Stacy. With it being abundantly clear that he's going to keep telling me his name and job position until I acknowledge it, I say, "Yeah, um, the name's—José."

"José? You don't look Mexican."

"Oh! Well, my dad was… um… *not* Mexican—from Cancun! And my mom always loved the name José. Said it sounded romantic—like a foreign car or something. And she really liked Tequila. Said she never made a decision without it."

"Oh, thank goodness! I was nervous you might be black or Mexican or a rapist when you pulled over. You have an indefinite look."

I consider explaining that my "indefinite look is thanks to having a black father and white mother and that I wouldn't recommend grouping black and Mexicans with rapists, but the conversation feels too elevated for a roadside breakdown. Instead, I say, "So you haven't answered me, yet. What happened to the car?"

"Well, it's the kookiest thing. All of a sudden the radio went out, the gauges dimmed, and then nothing." He walks to the side of the car and kicks the front driver's side tire. "Air seems fine, though."

He's wearing leather loafers—the kind guys on yachts wear when they're vacationing in the Mediterranean. And Big Hurry's wearing them with an *"I'm With Stupid* →*"* T-shirt and using them to kick adequately inflated tires.

"It's probably your alternator," I say, trying my damnedest to avoid the subject of the amount of air in the tires. I walk over to the driver door and lean into the car through the window; I lean, instead of opening the door, so as not to arouse Big Hurry's suspicions. The interior of the car is gray, freshly vacuumed, and clean, except for a couple of empty water bottles scattered at the foot of the shotgun seat, and two more unopened bottles of water sitting on the seat. Turning off everything electrical—the radio, air conditioner—I turn the ignition off and pull the keys out. Walking back to my car I say:

"I'll pull my car around and give you a jump."

"Gee, thanks! You sure are a saint, José. God is good. I always tell the kids—*God is good.*"

I feel my jaw clench and my neck muscles tighten. Yes, of course, God's will was to leave me stranded at a stoplight and then to leave you stranded on the side of a mountain road. God is good, indeed. Pulling my car around, I contemplate the possibility that maybe Big Hurry's car just overheated. Could be. Given his ignorance of proper car maintenance, I wouldn't be surprised if he didn't understand that you were supposed to check the water and radiator fluid. Hell, I wouldn't be surprised if he didn't know that the internal combustion engine runs on gas. I stop my car after a brilliant three-point turn, step on the emergency brake, and get out. Before I bother with the jumper cables, I check the level of radiator fluid and water mixture. Somewhat ashamed that I hadn't noticed it before, I look up and say to Big Hurry:

"You don't have a drip of radiator fluid in here. Do you have any water?"

He looks at me with his face blotched by the same expression that I'd seen in the rearview mirror as I pulled over: "Are you going to rob me for my Evian?" it asks.

But then, suddenly sobered, his shoulders slink down and his face narrows, but only for a second, because the next instant he smiles, *joyously*, like a man who has just glimpsed his newborn daughter for the first time and for a precious few moments there is only joy and relief before a lifetime of worry. I've lived my life up until this moment striving to be the alpha male that my football coaches and the cinema told me I should be, but suddenly, looking at Stacy—this simple father who is rushing to be with his daughter for some trivial event she's not even going to remember in two weeks—I realize, well, for one that we are not wolves, and for two that until recently I wasn't even the alpha in my apartment.

Big Hurry says: "Yeah, I've got some water. Are you thirsty?"

I smile and shake my head. "No. It's for the radiator. Usually, you should have fifty-percent water, fifty-percent radiator fluid, but in a pinch you can just use water. Let's get you to that game."

I realize that maybe his daughter won't remember the game, but emotionally she'll always remember that her dad was *there*. Suddenly, the gridlock I had felt when I had first seen Big Hurry on the side of the road clears up, and an intoxicating self-satisfaction and inordinate pride rush through me. His daughter will remember him, and he'll remember me, maybe not until death, but for a long time I will be a fixture in his memory, popping in here and there, haunting him every time he travels the Crest. My place in his mind will last even longer than his shoes—though I'm sure it won't be nearly as comfortable.

He hands me a bottle of water, and I pour it into the radiator. Suddenly he grabs my hand and shakes it greedily. "Thank you. Thank you *so* much. Take these."

I look in my hand and see the treasure he has given me—playoff tickets. "You don't want to give these to me. These, God, these are worth your weight in silver right now. Everyone's trying to get them."

"I want to give them to you," he says, without a hint of hesitation or doubt in his voice.

I'm conflicted—would accepting his charity, any charity, even a gulp of water for my parched mouth, throw Karma out of balance? My father used to tell me: "A man in balance will know peace; a man out of balance will know retribution." But I had always dismissed it as a piece of religious dogma, a fear tactic used to curtail the forbidden excesses of youth. I was never able to understand the depths of its meaning, until now. For once, I decide to listen to my father and strive for balance.

"Take your daughter to the game," I say. "Tell her you're making up for being late to her game."

He smiles. "I'll tell her they're compliments of the friendly stranger José."

"My name's not José. Just say the Friendly Stranger." I nod and get back in my car.

Big Hurry continues to look at me, his hands on his hips, smiling as if in amazement. The sun vanishes behind the mountains and shadows fall. I make a three-point turn and step on the accelerator, leaving Big Hurry behind. A smile smears across my face so quickly that it makes my cheeks ache and my eyes water. I howl into the steering wheel as "Highway to Hell" plays triumphantly on the radio. Hoisting Big Hurry's keys, I begin to cackle. In my rearview mirror I can see, now probably half a mile behind me, the blue Infiniti, but not Big Hurry, and I know he's inside, frantic, probably crying or at the very least near tears, mystified as to what happened to his keys. *The Friendly Stranger couldn't have taken them.*

But where the H.E. double-hockey sticks are they? A fresh attack of cackling overcomes me, and I swerve nearly off the road; tires squeal, the car fishtails, but I steady the wheel and continue surging forward. Rolling down my window, I think about the man I was on the road to becoming so long ago. And I remember my father's favorite saying, "Tithing doesn't just mean giving ten percent of your paycheck to the Lord—it means giving ten percent of *yourself* to Him. Think of it as a deposit for those times when He carries you." And I remember how one day my dad just didn't come home after he tithed a hundred percent of his life when the Lord carried a truck head-on into his car as he waited at a red light. Suddenly my pride and euphoria are commuted to a bitter loneliness and utter contempt. I'm not with *Stupid* anymore. Severely unhappy with life, with myself, with circumstance—with *everything*—I hurl Big Hurry's keys down an embankment as deep into the woods as I can, giving them as tithing, to God.

LABOR PAIN

Tuesday, June 20, 2017

HER NOSE IS NO LONGER CROOKED. It took an exhaustive amount of work. Three months to be exact. But that's less than the four-month project plan and significantly under budget. Beauty is the result of timing, economics, and topnotch engineering—and I nailed all three. The doll that had looked like it was caught between a sneeze and casting a Bewitch-style spell is now as cute as the bottom dollar would allow.

I set the doll down next to a picture of Joey and realize for the first time that my son's nose is crooked. I must have known this before, but in the past three weeks I've seen him all of five minutes, so maybe my memory is a little fuzzy. It makes me wonder—is my nose crooked? Pinching my nasal bridge, I confirm that it's not. Joey must have inherited it from my ex-wife, and God knows no engineering is powerful enough to undo the effects of that force of nature.

The phone rings. It's my boss, Chris. Seeing his name on the caller identification immediately makes my chronic back pain throb. It's a little early for my second dose of codeine, but I toss a pill in my mouth and gulp it down with a slug of coffee. Answering the phone, I regret not taking a triple dose. Hell, I don't know if there are enough pills in the bottle to make dealing with Chris palatable.

He says, "Bryan, turn on your instant messenger." With his whiny voice and habit of holding the phone too close to his mouth, Chris sounds like a witch trying to beatbox.

Taking a longing look at the steam slipping from my coffee mug, I click the mouse a few times and turn on the instant messenger.

He instantly messages me: *Come to my desk!*

Our cubicles share a wall. The only thing separating our backs is a partition panel not much thicker than a thumb. Throughout the day, I can often hear him breathing deeply like he's trying to quietly give birth. Never once has he just spoken my name and asked me to come over. As I push my seat back, I regard the doll's stiff body. Thick wrists. Square ankles. Triple chin. It's a healthy baby with a straight nose. I take a deep breath, stand and start toward his desk. As soon as I round the corner, he bursts out of his cubicle and marches past me like the ghost of a Confederate soldier charging into battle.

I continue into his cubicle and sit down. The chair is small and flimsy and makes a folding chair seem luxurious. Immediately I regret not bringing my coffee; this is going to take a while—it *always* does. Although I know it has been taken down, the methodical ticking of the clock that used to hang in the factory suddenly fills my ears, each hand announcing its every movement with a crisp *tick*. I look over the cubicle. Everything is gray, from the carpet to the electronics, to the desktop, to the partitions, to the vacation calendar hanging by the entrance, straight up to the ceiling. Even the windows in the building are tinted so that when you look outside, the San Gabriel mountains, the trees, the people in their business casual attire, even the sun, are muted. There are a hundred shades of gray but nothing even remotely sexy about any of them. I sit, waiting, the phantom ticking keeping me company as I try to recall if I ever recognized that my son has a crooked nose.

Five minutes later, Chris returns. He has the forehead of a museum, the rosy cheeks and pointed chin of a pre-pubescent elf, and eyes that perpetually confess that he's on the verge of soiling his pants. As Chris sits, he douses me with the pungent scent of Old Spice cologne. He looks at his computer, his work phone, his cell phone, the stacks of loose papers, all with an expression of confused exasperation.

"Bryan," he says, squinting his beady eyes and pursing his lips. Inexplicably, whenever he says my name, it sounds like "Bartleby" to me. It's then that I notice that his cheeks are as red as a baboon's hindquarters during mating season: he's flustered. He begins to use the heel of his hand to rub away a halo of spilled coffee from his desktop—but it's a stain, and his hand is not made of bleach, so the result is just a ruffling of his comb-over. "Listen, I ran your time-card today—because I have to, that's what HR tells me. I don't want to, but if I don't, well, I can't don't, because HR tells me I *have* to. And, well, you and I both know you clocked in five minutes late. I know five minutes doesn't amount to anything, especially considering the long drive to work, battling traffic, trying to find parking, then hiking to your desk and turning on your computer. And I know you'll make it up at the end of the day—but our forefathers never promised us Five Minutes. And five minutes *is* five minutes. I think we can both agree on that."

I nod. He's right—five minutes *is* five minutes.

"This isn't the first time this has happened, either. And that's the rub. You see, there are laws and regulations HR puts out in the employee handbook, and if you read them, you'd know that being on time is an obligation. Why, I'd even call it a duty. I was even on time today! And when we don't perform our duties, well, that leads to a change in relationship status, and separation. You understand, right?"

I had stopped listening. "What? No. I don't understand."

"How can I say this another way?—we're going to have to exit you."

I ask with amazement: "Am I being fired?"

"No no no," Chris says, holding up his hands as if he's being surrounded by cops. "We don't use words like that here. HR tells me that it's best for everyone involved if we don't use any words that can be used to describe the operation of a gun."

My hands begin to shake and the pain in my back sears through the malaise of the codeine. Taking a deliberate breath to steady myself, I say, "I'm being *exited* for being a few minutes late?" My jaw clenches. "Being five minutes late didn't prevent me from finishing the doll project way ahead of schedule."

"Yeah," he says, nodding profoundly and glaring sideways at the coffee halo. His wispy auburn hair is swaying in the breeze from the air conditioning, patting against his barren scalp. "Just imagine what you could have done if you were on time."

Monday, May 29, 2017

When they stop the manufacturing line, the only sound in the factory is the ticking of a traditional wall clock. It's one of those round clocks with oversized numbers and black hands. Looks like it could be an emoji anyone under twenty wouldn't recognize. Executives are all for continuous improvement but never at the expense of the production of dollars, so I do most of my work after-hours or during lunch. The clock has been my companion on many a project. I walk the manufacturing lines, listening to the steady ticking. At some point, it stops sounding like a progression. One tick doesn't follow another; they all exist at once. It's when this happens—when the beginning and end merge and there is only sound—that I do my best work.

The nose is being molded in stress—that's it! When the design engineers added the third chin, they introduced pressure to the mold they hadn't accounted for. I scan the data I've been compiling for the past three months, then pick up a doll with a cracked nose followed by one with the crooked nose. A simple tooling change would alleviate the stress and leave the doll with the intended adorable button nose. To test out this theory, I update the program to add a small wedge on the inside of the chin, then fire up the manufacturing line. Gears and cylinders go into motion, the smell of hot plastic and oil fills the air, and then the line begins to flow like a rolling black river. Even through the steady mellow of the painkillers, I feel the tingle of excitement.

The doll comes out and begins moving down the line. Its chubby arms are raised in the air like it's begging to be held, and as I lift it off the conveyor belt, it is still warm to the touch. I examine its button nose. It's perfect! I can't put it down. The validation engineers will need to confirm the results, which leaves this doll to me. My son's eleven, so he's not much into dolls, but for some reason, I'm sure he'll appreciate this one. I decide I'll take it to him when I see him later in the week.

Gathering my things, it suddenly occurs to me that the ticking has stopped. I glance up at the wall where my companionable clock has always hung. Maintenance has removed it and is in the process of replacing it with a red digital clock. Numbers so big you can see them from across the factory. Red block digits that look like all eights when viewed from a particular angle. Numbers that morph into one another without sound.

"Hey, Sam," I call as I walk back to my desk. "Can I get the old clock?"

"We've already thrown it away, Bryan. You wouldn't want that thing anyway. It loses time."

I glance at the doll in my hand. So still. So timeless. I say, "I guess it outlived its usefulness."

Tuesday, June 20, 2017

Time is a freeway. In Los Angeles. At rush hour. So anytime between 5 A.M. and 10 P.M. It warps based on mass. Speeds and slows at the behest of light. Stops—in fact, is almost always stopped—and is a complete construction of man. I tell myself this when I'm running late. As I am currently. Late to see my kid because HR needed me to sign a mountain of paperwork to ensure I can't sue the company. And of course, traffic is relentless. Or is it unrelenting? I hold my breath and concentrate, trying to slow the clock. Ever since childhood I've thought that sheer willpower could overcome time, and for some reason holding my breath became the method for exercising that power.

A white Subaru wedges its way in front of me, blocking me precisely one car length from my exit. A pinprick of dull pain begins in my lower back and stretches its fingers up my spine. *It's okay,* I tell myself, chewing a codeine. Continuous Improvement Engineers are constantly in demand. I won't be out of work long. But—*fuck!* I just bought this cell phone, and things are going to be tight. If Joy, my ex, can hold off on this month's child support payment for a few weeks, I'll be fine. I'm sure she'll be okay with it. It'll just be a couple of weeks, maybe a month…

"You're late," Joy says, frowning as she buckles Joey into the backseat of her car.

I check the time on my phone. "Five minutes."

"Yes, *five* minutes, Bryan. But we got here twenty minutes early like decent people, so you're half an hour late."

"That's twenty-five minutes."

She glares at me with her hourglass figure contorted in such a way that I can't help but try to focus my peripheral vision to study her. "It takes a special kind of person to be that detailed yet completely oblivious to context. We call those people *engineers.*"

I can tell she's been thinking up that line for some time.

"I'm sorry, okay? I didn't get to see Joey during my last visitation. Please let me spend some time with him."

She purses her lips. "Why didn't you call?"

I stammer, shaking the cell phone in my hand. "We're talking about five minutes!"

"Yes, and we counted every one of them." Joy is nodding emphatically, and I can tell she's *really* thinking about me.

I try to keep calm. I can tell she'll let me have my time with Joey if I can play it cool, but I can feel the tension building in my veins. I just got fired, er, *exited*, for being five minutes late, even though I had just killed it at work, and now she is giving me a hard time for being a couple of minutes late! "Why is everyone so suddenly fucking concerned with five minutes?"

She shakes her head, scowling. "I don't know. Maybe if you lean out the process, you'll figure out a more efficient way of pissing me off."

Always this damn obsession with one minor thing or another! Never anything of consequence. Never a moment to sympathize with someone who is having an awful day.

"We are going on vacation for a couple of months. I'll call you when we get back to arrange your next visitation." My jaw drops. "I need your child support check on time this month, for once."

I nod. What else am I going to do? Ask for more time?

She slips into the car and begins to pull away. As she merges onto the freeway, I suddenly remember Joey's doll in my backseat. "Wait," I say under my breath, knowing damn well they can't hear me. I can feel the heat from the sun beginning to burn my neck. Sweat beads uncomfortably along my hairline, and the smell of smog and grilled burgers from the nearby McDonald's cause my stomach to turn. I sit down in the car—I didn't even get to say hi to him. "Two months…" I mutter to myself. It's not forever. I'll give him the doll when he gets back.

"Fuck, Bryan," I say to myself, twisting uncomfortably in the seat. "He doesn't give a shit about the doll."

Friday, January 31, 2014

"You could have called," I say as soon as I hear the front door squeal open.

Joy's brown leather backpack is slung over one shoulder; it is so fat with textbooks, papers, and computer equipment that it looks like a replica of the Venus of Willendorf. She drops it casually to the floor. "Traffic was bad today."

"We live in L.A. There's always traffic."

Finally, she looks at me. "What are you so snappy about?"

I try to keep my composure. There's no use diving into a fight that I know will end with me apologizing and feeling like an asshole, I know that, but I can feel frustration sucking up all the oxygen in the room like a wildfire. "I took this new job so we wouldn't have to struggle anymore," I say, fairly calmly. "It's a lot of work, and I've got deadlines coming out of my ass." Not so calm now. "It'd be nice if I could focus on my work for a change instead of playing single dad."

Joy corks her head. "Single dad? Because you had to pick your son up and spend time with him?"

"And make dinner. And do dishes. And clean up. And try to fit in updating schematics between playing superheroes."

I'm not looking at her. I fix my eyes and try to ground myself on the coffee table to stop myself from yelling.

"I'm sorry," says Joy. "I know you do a lot, and I don't tell you I appreciate you enough."

The smell of fried hot dogs lingers in the air. In the next room, Joey rustles through his toy box, dumping plastic train tracks to the ground. Even though I had just taken my codeine, the dull pain radiating from my lower back becomes unbearable in the silence; I pop another pill and gulp it down with a swallow of Miller Lite.

Joy is quiet for a moment. I know she's waiting for me to look at her, but I refuse to give her the satisfaction. She says, "I'm late."

"I know," I say, looking at the schematic on my laptop. "That's what we're arguing about."

"No," she says. "I'm—*late.*"

I try a smile but feel my face twist into a sneer. "Great. Just great."

"We talked about this," she says, steel returning to her voice. "I went off the pill months ago. Was your day really that bad?"

I burst to my feet, my back screaming in agony. "Maybe I can get another job? That way I can have two kids and two jobs I won't have time for. I'm a forty-year-old man, Joy. It should be okay for me to have a career."

"You're an asshole," Joy says, turning away.

"Wait." I am barely able to manage the words through the pain. "I'm sorry"—it almost seems preordained that this would happen—"I am happy. I'm just not handling the stress of this new job well."

Joy touches my hand. The pain in my back subsides, and the flame of my rage dwindles to embers. She says, "How is your back feeling?"

"It's fine," I say, sitting carefully back down. "I'm fine."

She kisses my cheek. Her lips are so soft they feel like a warm cloud. "I'm going to change into some comfortable clothes. It's too early to confirm if there's a baby onboard yet. I'll take a test in a few weeks, but I think Joey may be getting that little brother he's so desperate for."

The euphoria from the double dose of codeine has begun to wash over me. My fingers tingle. The moments become wavy. Joy disappears down the hallway. The room feels alive—as if it's waking up around me.

"Daddy," Joey says, tugging my arm, stirring a brittle stick into a dream.

"Yes," I hear myself say.

He sits down next to me, wiggling his block feet. Leaning his head against my arm, I feel like I'm floating, like the world is all air, and we're bouncing about in a bubble. Joey says, "Daddy, I wish you were my age."

"Why?"—the word flutters away like dandelion petals in a gentle wind.

"So we can play together all day."

I smile. Colors are unfurling like streamers around me. Joey slips to the floor and begins building train tracks across the carpet. I gaze at the train tracks and imagine the five-year-old me laying on my stomach next to Joey, flicking my ankles like fish tails. I think: *That's what heaven must be.*

Tuesday, June 20, 2017

Cle-thuh.

It is the sound of a pill bottle opening. Scrape of plastic. Gasp of air. I can feel the sound waves ripple through my blood. Faintly—*I have taken too many.*

Humorless laughter in the breathlessness.

My back hurts when I sit up straight and when I slouch. Everything else is sludge. Semi-living mud with a spine whose every molecule aches.

Thack.

The bottle closes.

Cle-thuh.

The pictures of Joey seem to shiver. The world is waves and pain and shame and regret. The pictures fold around me, warping the room, stretching seconds, until there is only Joey's five-year-old nose. Crooked.

I hold my breath and squeeze the doll's leg. No sensation of touch. Just snap of plastic and escape of air.

All the pills in the bottle plunge into the sludge with a slug of whiskey.

Monday, September 22, 2014

We were exactly on time, which means precisely nothing. We add our name to the list and sit down in the waiting area. I don't know if I should scroll through a magazine, twiddle my thumbs, or put my head down. Five minutes pass and a nurse takes us back into the delivery room, directs Joy to change into a gown, and exits. Joy gives me a pensive glance. It's the first time she's looked at me since the morning. Five years of marriage and I think it's the longest she's ever gone without looking at me. Joy closes the curtain and changes into the gown.

Nine months, and here we are. Well, nine months and two weeks. Joy looks as uncomfortable as ever. Belly bulging like a parasitic funeral mound. Almost unrecognizable as the petite little thing I married. She scooches back onto the bed and places her hand on her belly for the first time in weeks. "Here we go," she says.

Her contractions became regular last night but were far enough apart that the doctor scheduled us to come in the morning. The delivery room has a sterile smell and is cool, almost cold. The nurse reenters and begins to fuss with a plastic sack and some buttons on the IV pole. She helps to position Joy in the stirrups, Joy's thin legs bent like tentacles holding up swollen ankles. "You're dilated to a nine so we won't need to induce labor. Please be patient while we finish getting everything ready. How far apart are the contractions?"

"Five minutes," I say; I've been obsessively checking them on my watch and noting the times.

"Are you opting for an epidural?"

"No," Joy says. I've also forsaken my codeine; it's as if both of us wordlessly agreed to bear the full brunt of today's pain.

The doctor enters the room wearing baby blue scrubs. She is a fifty-something Asian woman who doesn't look a day over twenty-five. "Please bring me the Doppler monitor," she says to the nurse as she sits down next to Joy. "How are you feeling?"

"Pained."

The doctor frowns pityingly, suddenly looking every year her age. The nurse hands the doctor a monitor that has a cord with an attachment that looks like a microphone. She squeezes an exact line of clear jelly on the microphone and presses it firmly into the side of Joy's belly. A faint echo like happy whispering begins to play on the speaker. I glance at the monitor, and even though I've carried the knowledge for two weeks the *zero* on the digital heartrate knocks the wind out of me. I look away. Outside the window, balding trees sway mockingly. I imagine the autumn snickering, dropping auburn leaves like fake tears. "Can we close the blinds?" I ask the nurse. "Please."

A few minutes later, the doctor says, "It's time. I'm going to break your water. You're going to feel like you need to bear down like when you have to go to the restroom." She makes an expression like bear claws with her hands. "Just remember to breathe through the contractions."

Joy grips my hand. "We're ready," she says.

The doctor hands the monitor to the nurse and stations herself between Joy's legs. "Okay, now. Push for me."

Joy pushes, squeezing the blood out of my hand. When she stops pushing, she gasps as if she's come up for air, her cheeks and neck flushed with bright red splotches.

"Remember to breathe."

Joy pushes again, contorting her body and pressing her face between her shoulders so that the skin around her neck folds into waves. It looks like she's being tortured and she's trying to rip her essential self out of her flesh to escape her captors. The smell of blood, feces, urine and something foreign that I can't describe fogs the room.

"Push!"

Joy grimaces, her lips curling. She unleashes a grunt that sounds like a long, foreboding growl. A vein emerges from her forehead, pulsing. Crow's feet span out from her eyes, spreading like cracks in the land during an earthquake. She is the body of agony. Agony that in all other cases is so noble but now is so fruitless.

"The baby is crowning," the doctor says.

It looks like a doll. Like someone has played a cruel prank on us and somehow placed a doll in my wife's uterus. It reminds me of the latest line of dolls they just began manufacturing at work, except this one doesn't have the crooked nose that's been giving the execs fits. This doll is perfect. The problem is that it is just a doll. It never had a heartbeat. We never felt it kick. We never read to it, sang to it, painted a room for it. We never named it.

"Would you like to hold the baby?"

Joy nods. She is fighting back tears. Sweat is dripping down her face, and there is snot on her lips. And she is the bravest thing I have ever seen. I know there is nothing that could ever happen that could make me love her less. The doctor hands her the naked baby, and Joy gently places him against her breast.

"He's still warm," Joy says, looking up with sudden hope.

The doctor regards her with a sad, knowing smile. "That's just from your body's warmth."

"Oh," Joy says, a tear shooting down her face. "Hi," she says to our child, examining his face. "It's so good to hold you, Victor. I'm your mommy. I'm so sorry I didn't do a better job."

"You didn't do anything wrong," the doctor says.

I touch her shoulder. "You did a perfect job."

"How do you think Joey is going to take it?" Joy asks, without looking up from Victor. "He wanted a little brother so bad."

"He'll be okay. When the time's right, we'll give him a brother."

"He looks like you," she says, succumbing to tears. "Do you want to hold him?"

She hands Victor to me, and as I hold I can feel the warmth of his body fading. I squeeze my windpipe closed with all my strength—trying to fight time, to stop it, to reverse it. I hold my breath so long I can feel the world dimming. Sound and light and touch melting into a defiant, silent blur. I hold my breath so long my knees buckle and I collapse to the floor. Air rushes back into my lungs. Pain shoots through my kneecaps straight to my corrupted back. And for a moment, through the hurt and the gasping and the haze and the weightlessness of my body and the little body in my arms, it feels as if time has been irreparably stunted.

A STUDY IN DISCONTINUITY

Annotation

Edward had ordered the feeding tube to be removed two weeks previously. It was a matter of minutes now, maybe hours, perhaps a day.[1] White against the white sheets and white walls and white floor, over the twenty-one years of her residence it had become increasingly difficult to articulate Christa from any other structure in the hospice. Still, it was hard to believe the room could exist without her. It was her presence that merged the unseen forces—the desires, the fears, the memories—with the artifacts in the room—the bed, the sheets, the bills.[2] The only color in the room was the pastel tangerine of a vase of California poppy[3] wildflowers Edward had set on her bedside table.

He rubbed his eyes,[4] sending sharp pains stabbing through his retinas and blurring his vision. Without his

---

1   He half expected her to awake—as if she viewed the removal of the feeding tube as a bluff she was determined to call.

2   The fact that he was still here felt like a great accomplishment, but at best it had amounted to a Pyrrhic victory for them both.

3   A drought-tolerant and self-seeding wildflower that blooms from late winter to early spring. Its stems can be used in medications for insomnia and depression, and its lobed petals only open in the sun. The annual bloom of poppies had given Christa's mother so much hope prior to her death.

4   It had been ten years since hers last opened.

glasses,[5] the world was all horizons. Carefully, he reached for the vase of poppies and held it up to his face. The flowers had an earthy fragrance and left a pungent taste on his tongue. He put the vase down and wrenched himself to his feet. Feeling his way to Christa's side, he sat on the edge of the bed and leaned down so he could see the entire topography of her face and feel her breath—acidic and rank—on his cheek. Moments later the steady beeps of the heart monitor extended into one shrill squeal.

Hypothesis

The entire history of the heart is preserved in its countless layers, disjointed only by quakes at fault lines fractured deep within its depths. Nothing that has ever crossed its face has been forgotten or lost. Past wrongs are absorbed and fossilized, only to be ripped out and used as fuel for future generations of hate and rage. Its internal processes never change—no matter how scarred and transformed the world appears there has never been any real transformation, just the predictable continuation of the unchanging forces within and laws that predate the birth of the universe.

Experiment

He remembered the first time Christa's consciousness resurrected from her vegetative state—it felt like a practical joke. Her mother's ecstatic voice burst with emotion

---

5   He had spent the morning studying her hollow face so intensely that it had strained his eyes. Compulsively he began to rub his eyes from beneath the glasses—in his revelry knocking the glasses to the floor.

as she told him about how she had asked Christa how she was feeling, and Christa had responded: "Hungry." As he drove to the hospice, he relived the night of Christa's accident time and again.[6] After he'd parked, he sat in the car clutching the steering wheel. Just days before he'd finally felt like he was moving on—like the guilt and shame had passed, and he was ready for a new stage in life. His fingers ached as he squeezed the steering wheel—he had decided he was going to file for divorce and politely inform her parents that they would have to arrange for her care going forward, and then suddenly she was awake. Trembling, he let go of the steering wheel and went inside.

The first thing she said to him was—"I still remember you."

It had been five years since the crash.

He sat down on the edge of the bed. "You do?"

"Yes, I still remember *everything*," she said, her somewhat slurred speech cool and unaffected. Although her voice was wispy, hoarse and labored, it was still unmistakably Christa's.[7]

"I'm glad you're awake."

She was looking out the window, her rose-brown eyes so vivid they were almost iridescent on her face. On a dresser next to the window was a vanity mirror which had been turned around to face the wall. "You look old," she said, her eyes fixed on the window. "Not *older*. Just old."

---

6   Lying next to him, Sarah had never even seemed to consider slipping on a robe. Instead, she lay on the bed, every inch of her bare, as the police officer told Edward what hospital Christa was being taken to. As he walked out the door, she kissed him and told him to take care of his wife.

7   Edward had never heard her mispronounce or mumble a word. She had always spoken with such precision and clarity that it seemed like her every word had always existed. Now, even without the crisp diction, her words still felt preordained.

"I love you," he managed to say.[8]

"Love?" she scoffed. "I suppose that's why you were in such a hurry to get here." She swallowed, took a deep breath. "It's so frustrating to have to learn to speak again just to talk about the same old things."

He looked at the mirror facing the wall.[9] "Then let's talk about something else, dear."

"I like the sound of that—*dear*. Yes, call me dear from now on."

"Yes, dear."

"You know, Mother tells me that I've been in a coma for more than five years." She took a furtive glance out the window. "It feels like you walked out yesterday." She reached over to the nightstand and picked up a paper plate with a piece of what looked like wedding cake on it. "I can still smell the beef jerky you were gnawing on. I'm glad you walked out—I am. But now it's like I've awoken to you in the morning and nothing has changed but everything remains."[10] She took a bite of the cake and set the plate on her lap. "This is awful."

"Would you like me to get you something else?"

"*Dear*—call me *dear*."

"Anything you want, dear."

"What happened to the arrogance you were known for? You've become such a bore. Really—no girl could ever love you now."

He looked at her, all his old classifications of her winding through the once dry rivulets in his mind. She was

8   *but it's time to move on,* he couldn't manage to say, his will suddenly deflating.

9   He couldn't see himself saying the words, not now, not like this.

10   Nothing can expire in the absence of time. He had lived through all the consequences—the pain, the regret, the guilt—and had finally come to acceptance and forgiveness of self. She hadn't experienced any of that. And at that moment he understood what he had done to her.

harder than before; yes, her muscle tone and curves had softened, but her manner had hardened and the luster of her once youthful radiance had metamorphosed into a black sheen that was fractured in so many directions that it left only the thin cleavage of her current sadism. Yet here she was, against all probability. It had to be for some reason greater than scorn. He felt his hands squeeze into fists so tight his fingernails dug into his palms. "I know, dear."

"Is your research whore[11] waiting for you at home?"

"No," he said. "She left years ago[12], dear."

"You remember when you wrote that paper about your beloved Discontinuity?[13] The one she made that joke about? What was it?—'what does a pimp say to get the party started?'"

Clenching his jaw: "*Mo ho*, dear."

"*Delightful.* Yes, that paper. That's when you were worthwhile."

"I wrote that a long time ago, dear."

"I bet my ordeal is quite the financial hardship[14] on you."

"You're not a hardship, dear."

She glared at him. "You must be straight with me from now on." It was clear on her face that her vocal chords were strained and it was painful for her to articulate the words, but the fierceness in her eyes revealed how determined she was to speak. "The doctors have no idea how I've come back and say I could slip back any minute, so I don't want

---

11   Sarah. She became his research assistant the summer before the accident.

12   Shortly after the accident, she accepted a role in a survey of the evolution of rocks at the Carnegie Institute of Science.

13   Mohorovičić discontinuity. The boundary in the earth between the crust and the mantle where seismic waves accelerate.

14   After insurance coverage, $74,005, and counting...

to waste any time with pleasantries. All I ask is for a few moments"—swallow, deep breath—"of honesty."

He released his grip. "It's been a hardship."

"Good. I want to keep it that way. I don't want my family[15] to be burdened with the bills. I plan to continue living in whatever state I must until science can clone me an eternity of noons." Her voice was so slurred that as she said "noons" it came out as a hiss. "I hear you when you talk to me, you know." She smoothed the sheet on her lap and looked out the window. "Oh, I can't remember the words or the sentiment, nor do I care to. In your current state they'd probably just bore me anyway—no wonder I've been asleep so long!" She took a drink of water and looked back at Edward. "But your voice—so small and weak in the darkness—does offer some amusement."[16]

"What's it like, when you're—*in-between?*"

"Dear," she asserted.

"Dear," he repeated.

She looked at him, her sharp, luminous eyes peering out of the soft mass of her body. Despite the weakened state of her body, she held herself in such a regal manner that in retrospect her awakening seemed inevitable, almost preordained. Meanwhile, Edward sat on the edge of the bed, his sinewy frame slouched over, almost collapsing in upon itself.

"You wonder if it's a miracle that I came back from Bermuda?" she asked, a disjointed, snide grin beginning on her uncooperative lips.

He nodded [17], dust-gray eyes examining the tile floor.

15   Net worth: $22.9 million.
16   Her words echoed in his memory as if the words of a bully mocking him year after year.
17   He couldn't vocalize the words. Seeing her—hearing her— triggered such profound doubt.

"Oh my—this is interesting. You—the devout scientist—*believe* that my awakening was a miracle." She stretched out her neck. "The very word is blasphemy to your science—yet you *believe?*"

"I want to."

She leaned towards him and whispered: "What would you have me ask if I am to slip back?"

He looked up at her[18] and asked: "Are we more than just biology?"

"More than science?" she asked, glowing with sardonic glee. "Oh, Edward, you and your science crucified God long ago. There's no one for me to ask."

Origins

He imagined it had begun at the friction between fault lines, and over time they had steadily spread apart, eventually leaving only the shared scar of the coasts where they had once been united. Mountains, canyons, lakes are created by friction, but whose *fault* had it been? Did it even matter anymore? The Pangaea[19] of their union had split so long ago that only if he pieced together the continents of his memories was it even recognizable. They had evolved into different worlds; only scars and distance remained now, but the forces that created those scars and expanded that distance were still churning below, unchanged and immutable.

---

18   As he looked at Christa's battered face that night in the emergency room, he could still smell Sarah on his fingers. It was all so illogical—the primal, bestial machinations of it all. And that disturbed him far more than the discoloration and swelling of his wife's face. It was the first time he'd ever felt a yearning for something more. He just kept asking himself the one question that would go on to undermine his career and ignite a silent crisis within him…

19   The supercontinent that existed when all the earth's continents were united, 300 million years ago.

When he first met Christa, his entire life had been transfigured by the golden luster of her skin and the sheen of her rose-brown eyes. He dug himself out of his work and turned his attention toward examining the mysterious trenches of her personality. Even though she refused to discuss her past or her dreams for the future, her refusal just increased his hunger. With fervor, he studied the way she acted apathetically toward the world around her, while somehow also being affected by it to her core. There was the way she kissed and touched with such a precise order and timing that it seemed any deviation could cut her. And the way that after they'd made love, she would slip into her robe and sit at the edge of the bed, combing her black hair in long, deliberate strokes until every last knot was removed and any follicle evidence she had just been engaged in a romantic tryst was erased. He knew his career as a geologist would suffer, but he entrenched himself in her; she became his career. Even though part of him—the incorrigible scientist who dreamed only of new questions—had not been ready for the endeavor, he reconciled himself with the thought that "you don't walk away from a vein of gold simply because you're not ready to mine it."

Meticulously, he'd begun his excavation, surveying and plotting each movement, brushing back the sands of dissimulation and guardedness as he labored to unearth the antiquities within her. He yearned to know her darkest depths, the inner, unseen forces at work within her— the entire geology of her heart. Systematically he dug, searching for the vulnerabilities and passions that shaped her being, but he just kept unearthing the same jagged, routine nuggets with every excavation. Finally,[20] after

---

20   Sarah entered his class wearing a tank top and an eager smile. All that seemed to exist for her was future; the present and her new

three years, their home remained bare, and he resigned himself to the fact that his grand hypothesis was wrong and there was no soft, molten core—no vulnerability, no passion—just a cold, desperate need for control. And there never had been any gold.

Thanatopsis[21]

"She woke up again," Mary said with measured excitement the second time Christa awoke, two years after her first awakening. "Just woke up while I was telling her about how some poppies had bloomed in the garden."

Mary met him at the entrance to the hospice, and they took the elevator up to Christa's room together. She was holding a glass vase full of poppies, their closed bulbs slouching over the sides. As the elevator ascended, Mary jabbed him with what he must and mustn't do when he saw Christa. He *must* be delicate and kind with her; she always has been a sensitive girl, you know. He *mustn't* challenge or offend her. He must be careful not to patronize nor be too blunt with her. He mustn't try to press her or make her feel uncomfortable in any way; she remembers all the old things, you know. Most importantly, he must remember that every moment of her time is priceless and must be cherished. Edward stood in the elevator, sweating, his nerves churning, crushing, and changing his every thought and feeling.[22] Finally, as they exited the elevator and walked down the hallway to

professor were mere fascinations. Edward had never known a student so bold, so inquisitive, so utterly undiscovered.

21   A meditation upon death.

22   The metamorphic process of living—the constant heat and pressure giving life to shapes and characteristics never otherwise imagined.

Christa's room, Mary said, "You know, I could blame you for all of this, given that *escapade* you had with that student of yours. But I don't. Christa never was one to check her blind spot, so it was just a matter of time before it happened. You're a geologist; you understand matters of time. And that student of yours did have nice legs. Nicer than Christa's at her best. Christa always had the most extraordinary eyes, though. I've never seen another pair like them."

When they reached the entrance to Christa's room, Mary handed him the vase and said: "Telling her about the poppies brought her back—maybe being around them will keep her here. I'll give you two some time alone. Do remember what I said."

As he walked in, the sterile smell of the room was offset by the pungent smell of the poppies and a sweet smell he couldn't immediately identify. Then he saw it: slices of cake, each with at most a bite or two taken out of them, were stacked on the nightstand next to Christa. Christa was stretched out comfortably on the bed, looking out the window. Part of him hated her for coming back. He had vowed a hundred times not to let one night define him—not to be broken by his broken marriage and Christa's accident—but every time he felt like he could move on, the thought of her returning would surface, or, as was the case now, Christa would resurface.

"I'm glad you're back, dear," he said, sitting down on the edge of the bed.

She turned her head to look at him, her eyes so lustrous they were practically glowing on the ashen waves of her face.

"It's so dreadful what's become of me," she said without sentiment. Compared to her first awakening, her tone was softer and her voice more coarse.

He pursed his lips and looked away. "I know, dear."

"But so delightful that my coming back tortures you."

He set the vase on the windowsill and tried to focus on the world outside. "It doesn't torture me, dear."

"You're so impossibly uxorious now," she said, her voice breaking. She took a breath and composed herself, carefully readying herself to speak again. "You're like an indentured servant consoling yourself with lies of God, terrified of the terrible truth that there is only despair." She took a drink of water, a bite of cake. "I imagine your work has suffered."

He clenched his fists. His toes curled in his shoes. "Yes—it has, dear."

"I bet you've even prayed."

He nodded, lips trembling.

"Delightful. You know I remember all the old things."

"Yes, dear."

"Even better than before."

"I know, *dear*."

"You scoundrel."

He whipped around, holding out his hands, eyes wide. "It all happened so long ago."

"Your past is my present—do you understand that?" She took a sip of water, then stabbed a fork into a slice of cake, where she left it without taking a bite. "I imagine you fancy me an oracle now."

"No, dear."

"Go on! Roll my bed to Delphi, and perhaps I will bring something back with me."

"I'm just glad you're back, dear."

"I'll go back soon enough, and you'll go back to praying."

He swallowed. "I will."

"Now it's me that sees that there is no God while you pray to Him?"

"I do, dear."

"Ironic." She massaged her throat, then took another sip of water. "I've scoured the entire breadth of my existence—my subconscious is as familiar to me as metamorphic intrusions are to you—and all I've found are endings. No light. No angels. Just a beckoning blackness. And yet you say your asinine[23] prayers?"

"I do."

"You drop coins into a bottomless well."[24]

"Yes."

"Science—it brings you no comfort anymore?"[25]

"No."

She seethed: "What about your crucified God?"

He didn't answer. He stood there looking at her, trying through rational thought to relieve the pressure of the humiliation and fury swelling within him, filling his every pore with sweltering rage until finally the words frothed out of his mouth—"I'm going to have them remove the feeding tube when you slip back."

"No, you're not." Her tone was cool, dismissive.

He exhaled, in doing so finally realizing that he had been holding his breath. "I know, dear. I'm glad you're back, dear."

"What a pathetic little gnat you've become—completely unworthy of love and scorn alike. It's as if I'd run you over on my way to that infernal car crash." She took a long drink of water and then casually dropped the glass to the tile floor. "You used to be this brash scientist—somehow both scholarly and artistic while immersed in your sacred scientific method." She coughed hoarsely into her shoulder. "Why, even after your scandal, I couldn't fault

---

23   They make more sense than our asinine vows, dear.

24   There are no coins left to drop, dear.

25   Your eternal silence would be my greatest comfort, dear. Dear. Dear, dear, deardeardeardeardeardeardeardear—*dear*!

the sincerity of your character. You remember what you said after I caught you? You said: 'I wouldn't be the first prospector[26] to mistake iron disulfide for gold.'

"Pyrite is the geological name, right? Fool's gold, Edward! How perfectly you summed up your images!" Her voice was so hoarse now that her words eked out in whispers and dry croaks. "But now—look at you. Oh, on second thought don't bother; you'll see the same thing either way. I wonder… tell me, how would you describe me now?"

He opened his mouth to speak but couldn't form the words. He was left trembling, staring at the floor.

"What a pity," she said, looking back out the window. "You lost everything you ever had, only to find out there's nothing else."

Without taking another look at her, he left.

Survey

According to Christa, it was two years after their wedding that Edward's attention drifted and settled so completely on his research.[27] The hours he had spent examining her became devoted to a new subject,[28] a subject separate from her that required nothing of her. Christa wrote:

> Seeing that you no longer find it necessary
> to slither home, I no longer find it necessary
> for you to have a fully stocked library. So if

---

26   Rest assured, Edward, as far as that student of yours is concerned, you weren't the first prospector to mine that ore.

27   —Whore.

28   The sun-bleached skin of Sarah's arms and legs, the pale crescent of her abdomen—the sway of her round hips and red hair as she rocked back and forth atop him.

you're looking for any of your sacred texts, follow the smoke trail. Fire both destroys and renews, right? So maybe your studies will have renewed meaning to you now. And maybe your constant "fieldwork"[29] will come to an end.

When I married a geologist, I should have known he would have the emotional maturity of a stone, but I could have never imagined you would leave me in an empty bed so many nights. And the last time you did share a bed with me, as I lay next to you, thinking we had finally reconnected, I asked you what you were thinking, and you launched into a dissertation about some coffin-shaped crystals that were discovered in a cave worlds away. And you couldn't understand my outrage—why should you be expected to be thinking the same things at the same time as me? But I was lying next to you NAKED, Edward! And you were thinking about rocks, geological functions. What about biological functions? What about your wife?

Our marriage is fracturing.[30] In one of your textbooks, I happened upon the definitions, and the term "Recolonization"

---

29   Surveying a rift valley, Sarah said: *Question—how would you respond if I kissed you? Hypothesis—by promptly undressing. Experiment—fuck you, and observe the change in my test scores.*

30   His relationship with Sarah suddenly clouded everything. It wasn't that they saw something in each other—it was what they didn't see, the veil of blackness illuminating every sensation as they groped about in the darkness. He didn't care about how she anticipated a laugh—the corner of her lips twitching, her misty blue eyes wet and alert. And she never laughed when he treated the most frivolous matters with such

called out to me... [it means] a second or renewed colony. It's your choice; you can choose to create a second colony with her or renew your colony with me.... Your behavior, though sickening, is something I should have expected from a scientist. Love is not a logical progression but an irrational compulsion, so I don't expect you to love me because you're not suited for such things. But it occurs to me that you are true to your science and that at least offers hope for you... and for us.... I will be home tonight at 7:30. Bring home a bottle of sauvignon blanc[31] and examine me as you once did, if you wish to renew your studies.[32]

As their marriage eroded and the distance grew between them, Christa's tactics morphed from cool scorn and property destruction to an endless barrage of outlandish actions.

Her chief complaints were:

- The yard looks like an Amazon tribe lives in it;
- You forgot to take the trash out, pay the gas bill, fix the runny toilet;

---

gravitas that he became inadvertently funny. They knew nothing of each other—and it was precisely that ignorance that made their every touch so thrilling.

31   Christa owned and operated a boutique specializing in high-end cakes and expensive wines. One of her earliest "projects" had been to teach Edward how to pick out an exquisite bottle of blanc.

32   Green, Christa. A letter left on Edward's nightstand. 19 April 1990

- Your underwear drawer has been open for two weeks;

- How am I to do the laundry with your socks inside out?

- Your clothes, your Jeep, your briefcase, reek of sweet perfume and Snickers bars;

- Tell me, Edward, are you having an affair with a woman or a candy jar?

Her methodology consisted of:

- Christa, this is absurd—where did you hide the alarm clocks? It's 3:00 A.M. I have class at 8:00. Goddamnit, this is the third time tonight these damn alarms have gone off!

- When you have a moment, could you tell me what exactly is covering the yard? *The cotton entrails of all the stuffed frogs you have ever given me. I searched and searched, but I never found a heart inside any of them.* I hope you're feeling better after your tantrum. *No, but I feel better now that the sprinklers are on.*

- Christa, where are my keys? Jesus, are we playing hide-and-seek with my things again? Oh, this is great—you didn't just hide my wallet and keys, you also hid my underwear.[33]

---

33   *So she hid your underwear. That means if I were to reach my hand down here I'd find...*

He resorted to:

- Hi, it's Edward. I'm going to be working late, so I won't be home until after you're asleep. I have a lot of papers to grade. Just wanted to let you know.

- I'll see you in class this afternoon. If you want to see me during office hours, I'll save you a place on the couch.

On April 20, 1990, Edward came home late from the field and entered the house through the kitchen, eating a Slim Jim. Swirling a glass of pinot grigio, Christa commented that he was drinking a meaty glass of wine. She continued:

"It is unbearable to wake up reeking of her—unbearable! If you choose to amuse yourself in this way any further then I am ready for this to end, Edward. All of it."

She was sitting with her neck outstretched above her glass, looking at the fire softly crackling in the fireplace. Edward sat down on the arm of the couch, still chewing the long, red stick of his Slim Jim. He countered:

"There was a sag pond[34] by my house when I was growing up. One day I was playing on the bank when I happened upon a frog coming out of the water. It made such an effortless transition from water to land

---

34   Lake Una—a small bottomless lake created by the fault line of the San Andreas, reputed to be haunted by the ghost of a fisherman who lashes out at anyone who approaches.

that I marveled at it for weeks. I was seven, and I became obsessed with uncovering the mystery of it. But you know what? After I learned its secrets, after its amphibian behavior ceased to be such a marvel, I stopped studying it. There was no need. It wasn't the frog that inspired me—it was the pursuit of knowledge."

He ripped off a hunk of meat with his teeth and chewed with his mouth open for a moment. Casually, he concluded:

"You were just the latest wart-covered frog."

Edward observed her lips part almost imperceptibly. Her pupils constricted into black dots no larger than a nerve ending, and a shallow breath of air escaped her lips. It was a completely unknown expression to him—an absolute mystery—but rather than filling him with a lust to know the internal processes behind it, all he felt was a momentary curiosity. After a few moments of silence, Christa responded:

"I expect you to leave now."

Edward stood up, popped the last bite of Slim Jim into his mouth, then crumpled up the wrapper and shoved it in his jean pocket. Still gnawing on the processed meat, he kissed Christa on the cheek and whispered into her ear:

"I'll be on my way, dear. I have *research* to do."

As he left, he heard a wine glass shatter against the wall.

Pruning

The last time Christa awoke, Edward brewed a pot of coffee and stood in the kitchen drinking it until it was empty. It had been four years—four years of reliving their conversation and the hollow thud of his retreating footsteps. She'd been alive—truly alive—for just seven days in eleven years, and yet he couldn't stand to be in her presence for even that long. Setting the empty pot back in the coffeemaker, he stared at it listlessly. He didn't want to see Christa, but he knew that this was his final pursuit—that Christa, and his connection to her, was all he had left to study.

The first thing he noticed as he hobbled[35] into the room were the poppies beside Christa's bed. Mary was next to her, telling her about her father's recent activities, and Edward was immediately struck by the necessity of the lie. Her father had died three years before, but Christa had been unconscious for all of that time; with her time being so scarce her mother didn't want her to spend it grieving?

"Hello, dear," he said, quaking. His knees felt like they were swollen with an acid as thick as glue.[36]

She didn't answer. She just looked at her mother with her prismatic eyes, the expression on her chalky, toneless

35   Gouty arthritis: a painful buildup of uric acid in the joint resulting from the body's inability to expel purines adequately.
36   Once he'd felt the ache, it felt like the pain had always existed.

face as inscrutable as ever. The inflammation in his knees was so severe that he was forced to sit down in a plastic chair at the foot of the bed. Crouched over, rubbing his knees, he said, as if in reflex: "I'm sorry."

No response.

He continued: "I'm sorry about the last time. I shouldn't have walked out."

Again she just kept looking at her mother's weathered face, which had aged so heavily since her last awakening that it must have seemed foreign to her now.

"Dear?"

She said to her mother, "So father is well?" Her voice was frail and wispy and came out in strained croaks.

"Oh, as well as you can expect, considering he's an old man with pneumonia."

"I would like to know if something was to happen to him."

"Of course, dear. I wouldn't dream of keeping you in the dark about something like that."

"I should have complete honesty."

"Of course, dear—of course."

Christa had a piece of marble cake with white frosting on a Styrofoam plate sitting on her lap. She took a small bite, then set the fork down and placed the plate on the nightstand, where four other plates of partially eaten cake sat. "Doesn't anyone in this town make a good cake anymore?"

For a moment he considered going out and ordering cakes from every bakery in a twenty-mile radius; at least he'd have an excuse to leave.

Mary stood up and walked past him to the door. Still rubbing his knees and wincing, he heard Mary's voice whistle from behind him—"Edward, would you be so kind as to join me for a walk down the hall?"

He looked up at Christa; her rose-brown eyes were fixed on the poppies. With considerable effort, he stood up and followed Mary out the door.

"I dare say Christa's health looks better than your own," Mary said. "What have you been occupying yourself with these days? I hear you're no longer at USC."

"I'm teaching at Antelope Valley College now."

"The junior college? I bet the legs there aren't as long."

"Their legs are plenty long enough to take them where they want to go."

"I bet they're taking them *everywhere*," she quipped. "You were so ambitious when you married my daughter. I always thought that by the time you were a graybeard you'd be quite noteworthy, but instead, the only thing noteworthy about you is your ruin."

She walked on a little farther, Edward limping behind.

"She won't talk to you. After you walked out the last time, she refuses to even acknowledge your existence."

"I don't know what I'm doing here."

"We all know what you're doing here. Your legs might be long enough, but they're not well enough to take you where you want to go."

He stopped and bent over to tend to his failing knees. They were so inflamed that he couldn't bear to walk any longer.

"I won't lie to you and say that seeing you like this doesn't please me in some way. But it doesn't please me half as damn much as seeing you the way you were with my daughter when you were first married. She used to haunt your every thought—now, well, I guess she still does." Mary walked away, disappearing down the hall behind a wave of young nurses in green scrubs.

Throughout the rest of the afternoon and into the evening, Christa and Mary discussed updates on current events and family—the entire time neither of them so much as acknowledging Edward. As the earth turned away from the sun and faced out into the blackness of the universe, Mary kissed and hugged Christa goodbye for the night—crying the entire time—while Christa sat stoically. Edward remained—it was his right as a husband to spend the night. For hours she just sat there silently looking at the black window with an expression almost like longing. At some point, she fell asleep with her hands crossed on her lap. Edward watched her sleep for a while and then drifted to sleep himself.[37]

The next morning Edward stirred to the sound of a doctor talking to Christa. The sight of the doctor's blond hair and statuesque build was disconcerting because he wasn't the doctor from the emergency room that Edward had dreamt of. Edward half expected him to pronounce Christa pregnant and was unsettled when he didn't. After a few moments, Edward's conscious separated from his subconscious, and he was once again acutely aware of the stiffness in his lower back and the swelling in his knees.

The doctor scheduled a myriad of tests. The testing had nothing to do with finding a way to keep her from lapsing back into a vegetative state. They were to be performed purely for scientific discovery: to gather data, to form hypotheses, to reference in research papers to improve a few doctors' popularity—referred to as "esteem" in academia. Christa was a miracle, after all—expressed in a paper as a scientific singularity. How or why she unexpectedly vivified for days at a time before slipping back into the underworld of her stasis was a mystery.[38]

---

37   He dreamt that he was making love to Christa exactly the way she was now. As he delicately moved atop her, the clarion ring of a distant heart monitor chimed with the rhythm of their bodies. Immediately after they were done, the doctor came into the room and informed them that Christa was pregnant and would never slip into the abyss again.

38   After her second awakening, Christa's physician began

The day trudged forward: Christa talked with her mother, ate and drank nothing but cake and wine, rolled through the hospice garden in her wheelchair, did some more testing, and ignored Edward completely. A local news station showed up to do a story on Christa and her mother. Christa extolled the virtues of forgiveness and thankfulness, and Mary spoke about her struggle to maintain her faith during all those silent years as she dutifully exercised her daughter's arms and legs. Unexpectedly, they asked Edward how he had remained so steadfast. His eyes darted to the anchorwoman's legs, then to Christa. He responded: "There's no moving forward without her."

The next day went on the same—silence, indifference, isolation, despair. There were moments of bitter regret: Christa recounting the moments before the accident. Swatting at a fly. Not checking her blind spot. She never did. It was just a matter of time. There was anger: *Mother, can you do something about the stench. It smells like rotting old men in here.* And there was disbelief, numbness, a wild fantasy of scolding Christa for every wrong she had ever committed against him. Hatred, rage, compassion, sorrow—all of it churned inside of him until Christa fell asleep during her window vigil. Edward watched her as she slept and was startled to see her eyes, waxen and glossy, suddenly looking back at him. He knew she was conscious but sinking away. And in that instant, he knew that she'd risen again solely to hurt him. He'd mourned her death three times now—why should she never grieve? He said, "The poppies are from your father's grave."

comparing her to a woman in Colorado who had also experienced "cyclical awakenings." The doctor's theory was that because the brain requires the most resources to run, during her periods of stasis energy was building up until there was enough in reserve to power the conscious mind. No hard data exists to support this.

Did she smile, or was it just the involuntary contraction of the muscles in her cheek? A twitch? A cramp? He couldn't tell. The next second, she was gone.

Abstract

As the heart monitor squealed, Edward ran his hands through Christa's hair, extricating whatever knots he could. What had he expected? Some chance at redemption? A glimpse into the inner workings of creation? Christa had told him there would be nothing of the sort, and she had never lied. All she had ever asked for was honesty, and all he had ever given her was theory. He had studied her—studied the inner workings of the world—but as he attempted futilely to detangle her hair, he realized he had never looked inside himself.

Suddenly Christa's eyes flickered open, ablaze with wonder, full and vivid and alive! She looked at him, breathless and confused, with eyes that had never counted a moment.[39] Her dry lips parted to cry out, but her uncooperative vocal chords could only manage disjointed gasping.

Edward pressed his face to her cheek:

"You asked me once how I would describe you. It took a lot of years, but I finally have an answer. You're the layer between things where creation is neither molten nor solid and every disturbance is intensified. And no matter how hard I tried there was never any way I was going to reach you because I never knew where I was starting from. You're a discontinuity, *dear*."

---

39   Not the three years of their relationship before the accident. Not the five years to her first awakening or the two years until her second or the four years to her final awakening and the ten years to her rising now just in time to witness her death.

She grabbed his hand,[40] and her touch forced him to reject every theory he'd ever proposed. "You are my life's work"—he interlocked his fingers with hers and looked her in the eyes—"but it's time we both stop studying."

Her eyes floated away from his face. Trembling, he inhaled her last breaths, mesmerized by the radiance of her iridescent gaze, trying his best to decipher her sounds, until from the gurgling and choking and dying bloomed the word *"noon"* in one final, hoarse gasp.[41]

---

40 The day they met—after a morning surveying for a housing development, he'd happened into her boutique to pick up a cake for a surprise birthday party for the dean. He was about to leave when he saw the prices, but then he saw Christa. She asked if he needed help, and he gave her his best smile and leaned towards her, placing his dusty sleeves on the counter. She regarded his smile for a moment with an enigmatic expression, looked at the layer of dust and small rocks next to a sample wedding cake, and told him if he wanted to get his rocks off he'd have to get them off her counter. Then she touched his hand, just for a moment, and he felt the urge not only to get to know her but to become a part of her. It was the moment that inspired his paper on the Mohorovičić discontinuity: the moment the compulsion to create ceased to be about creating change in the next generation, and instead became about becoming the medium for change.

41 Every day Christa took lunch at precisely noon, and shortly into their courtship, Edward began meeting her when he didn't have an afternoon class. Their first fight occurred when he showed up five minutes late to one of these dates. Christa told him that if he couldn't respect her time she could never trust him to respect her. The next day when she stepped into her office for lunch, Edward was on one knee. "I'm a geologist," he said, "so I know a thing or two about rocks." He opened the ring case. "Marry me, Christa. I want to spend the rest of my life cherishing your every waking moment."

TEETH

I WAKE UP with her teeth in my hands. A canine. A pre-molar. A bullet-shaped molar with a silver crown that glints in the piss-yellow light of dawn. Baby teeth—but none of us are ever truly babies anymore. I scratch my testicles, nose, ears. Rub the sleep out of my eyes, even though it had been there for less than two hours. A good night. I'm getting better. Not well yet, but no one can afford to be well anymore.

I brew a single cup of coffee because waste articulates loneliness. I take a drink. It is bitter and smells like hot urine and ammonia. I use the black-brown coffee as a backdrop for her tiny teeth, and the emptiness of the universe steams out around us, so black and hot that I can only keep my bearings by focusing on the white buoys of her teeth clumped together in a Ziploc bag. We can't put our kids in bubbles, but every day we put them in bags.

I fry some bacon, eggs. Haley had always hated bacon. *It burns my mouth, Daddy.* Can't afford to be daddy anymore. I sip coffee. Smoke a menthol cigarette. Passive-aggressive suicide. I hate living but am too spiteful with life to ask for it to end. I go to my room. My room—mattress on the floor, no sheet, one pillow, no case. White walls. Tin foil on the window. Closet full of metal jackets—two rifles, a .22 caliber and a .38 caliber.

One shotgun, sawed-off. Seven handguns. Three silencers. One elephant gun. Where my work shirts used to be there are camouflage uniforms, ski masks, sandbags. Where my wife's shoes used to be, cases of bullets are stacked in order of caliber. My wife—*ex-wife*. There is nothing current. There is only *ex*.

I take out a case of bullets, a Beretta pistol, desert camouflage pants and jacket, and a gray ski mask. I get dressed in the camouflage. I load the handgun and stuff it in my jacket pocket.

It is 5 A.M., time to start looking for work. Searching for work isn't difficult. You just have to know where to look. Every day pedophiles are pushed back onto the streets, and a new file is opened on the internet, complete with name, address and picture. It is a public service to close them. Public?—these monsters are a part of the public. So to serve the public, you must kill the public. Now I serve the public that never served me or these teeth. Haley's file is still open; it is time to start closing theirs.

I turn on the computer, open my map. There are already five philes marked to be closed. I add another. I won't be coming home. Can't afford home. Not anymore.

I pull on my hiking boots. I don't bother to brush my teeth. I imagine them decaying, falling out, and being added to the Ziploc bag. Haley used to giggle when she would race her daddy to see who could brush their teeth the fastest, minty foam dribbling down her chin. Now I hold her incisors in my hand like coffin lids, one of them splintered in half from her last moments before her *last* moments.

I grab my keys, leave. It doesn't take long to get to my first stop. The phile is leaving his house, walking out into the desert toward a pond. Lake Una—it smells like algae and wet trash. There is a glitch in his step; he looks like a horse dressed in drag. I follow him. For the first time, I enter the desert.

I call out—*hey*. There is nothing else to say. He stops, looks at me. And I have my hand on the cold metal in my jacket pocket—the taste of dust and decay in my mouth. *And I have these teeth!* These teeth Haley lost before she lost everything. These teeth I found before they found her, before they never found him. These teeth that used to chatter after her mom would finally coerce her out of the swimming pool, that used to grind when she slept, that beamed when her daddy would reenact Christmas stories to put her to bed. These teeth like the remnants of all light having been ripped apart. And I have these fingers that function and squeeze and squeeze and squeeze and squeeze! And I have these eyes to see the lake his dead body floats upon. And I have this mind to remember—the bottomless memory, the bottomless misery—my bottomless daughter, both of us reduced to teeth.

YEARS OF THE DOG

THE DOG had been passed down through three generations. Although there was no way of confirming, the best guess was that the dog was eighty-three human years old, which meant that he was 581 dog years old, a right biblical old age indeed. Sometime during the second generation, the dog had come into the possession of Yi, now deceased, who had taken to calling him *Gáu-Gung*, a mashup of the word for dog, "gáu," and paternal grandfather, "Gung-Gung." The name loosely translated to Puppy-pa, an apt nickname as by this time the dog had begun to be treated like puppy and elder all at once. Puppy-pa was such a treasure that when Yi and his family fled Hong Kong as refugees during the civil war, they found a way to bring him over on *the boat*, at great personal risk and considerable effort to feed and clean up after the hound. No one could tell if it was apocryphal or not, but the family story was that in order to ease the family's burden, Puppy-pa had only peed the entire trip to America.

None of that was to say that Gáu-Gung hadn't aged. The dog, a mashup of a golden retriever, *shiba inu* and some type of bulldog, was said to have once been a tan color with reddish-brown patches, including one patch in the shape of a *9* and another that looked like an arrow.

But his face was now albino white, and the rest of his coat dusted as if he'd been dipped in sugar. Then there were the growths—thick bulbs of black flesh growing like ticks around his ears, lips, belly, and neck. They were the typical growths of an old dog, only exponentially increased in size and extent due to his remarkable longevity.

Over the years, Gáu-Gung had lived through a flood, a house fire, a home invasion robbery (that he slept through), and another flood. In fact, it seemed like floods followed the dog around, as every new place they lived seemed to flood within six months. For much of his life, Puppy-pa had a special affinity for water and swimming, but over the years that affinity began to wane as age, somehow, despite the incredible circumstances, began to affect the dog.

After Yi's death, his daughter, Jian, who had been in her twenties and had met her husband during *the boat* trip, took care of the dog for the next thirty-seven years. During this time, she raised one daughter—no boys—put the daughter through school, and watched her husband pass away, but Gáu-Gung persisted. The dog's health had begun to fade recently, however, a state of affairs that most distressed Jian. She took to treating the dog with ancient remedies, which thus far had only served to stink up the house and leave strange residues wherever the dog laid.

We need ginger, dragon fruit and salt, Jian told her daughter, who now went only by Jessica. I need you to take me to the market.

After forty-five minutes at the market, having traversed only three aisles and spent a considerable amount of time arguing loudly with a quartet of vendors, a process Jessica's mom described haughtily as "bartering," there was only one ginger root in the cart. The prices here are too high, Jessica's mom complained, hunched over a suspiciously overpriced ten-pound bag of salt.

Puppy-pa needs to be put down, Jessica said.

Jessica's mom cut her with a scathing glance in retort. With great effort, she hoisted the bag of salt and dropped it in the shopping cart. *Gáu-Gung* is family. You don't put down family.

Aye-yah, Jessica said in her broken Cantonese dialect. Every time she said anything in Cantonese, it reminded her mother of how American the family had become and the fact that her daughter had married and had a son with a *Yup-Boon-Jie*. She scowled as she remembered that the Japanese used to make sport of shooting dogs with arrows. At least he was a banker; she could respect him for that much at least.

The dog can't even lift himself up anymore, Jessica said, eyeing the bag of salt. There's no medicinal value to these so-called remedies you're trying. You're just prolonging Puppy-pa's agony.

So-called remedies? Jessica's mom shook the ginger root at her. These remedies have worked for a thousand years. You went to nursing school for two years and think you know so much. You do the math.

Jessica rolled her eyes—she was *always* rolling her eyes. The dog is miserable.

Would you put your *Poh-Poh* down, Jessica's mom asked, digging a fist into the salt.

It's like assisted suicide.

But not really, Jessica's mom thought, since a person has to be lucid enough to communicate their intentions to kill themselves, and Gáu-Gung, clearly having no ability to verbally announce his intentions or sign a release, could not be considered lucid enough to provide consent, so, no, *Jessica*—It isn't like assisted suicide. It is like grandma murder, which there's an English word for, believe it or not, *senicide*.

You and your google-searching is making me *senicidal*.

On reaching the house, Jessica's mom waved off all offers to help bring the salt, ginger root and dragon fruit—which had taken three stores to find an acceptable price for—into the kitchen. She turned on the wok, coated it with oil, and started to finely slice the ginger and dragon fruit. She added a cube of butter, then sautéed the ingredients until they turned into a thick paste, at which point she carefully poured the contents of the wok, which appeared to be half her size, into one of the many spaghetti sauce jars she had cleaned and continued to use throughout the years.

What was all the salt for? Jessica asked.

Dinner, her mom retorted curtly, dipping a finger into the concoction to see if it had adequately cooled.

After a few moments of silence, Puppy-pa, who had been laying in his customary spot next to the doggy door he no longer used, tried to get up but could only manage to straighten out his front legs; his back legs bowed and slid out behind him along the linoleum floor Jessica had insisted on running throughout the entire house. As means of complaint, Puppy-pa let out a low, hoarse whine and laid his chin on the floor. Jessica's mom hurried over to him with the spaghetti jar and strained audibly as she lifted Gáu-Gung to his feet. Jessica stood at the kitchen island, gritting her teeth.

Immediately upon reaching a feeble standing position, greenish-black bile loosened from Puppy-pa and plopped onto the floor like mud, splattering onto Jessica's mom's legs and slippers. Kissing the dog's head, she dipped a small, calloused hand into the concoction and told Puppy-pa—This will help you pee and digest your food. Now hold yourself up and eat. Don't pretend you can't stand.

The dog took a few weary licks of the substance before stopping and looking out at the nothingness around him with his kind, foggy white eyes.

You're Year of the Dog, you of all people should realize how special this dog is. Jessica's mom took a deep breath and began massaging the remedy into Gáu-Gung's boney, frail back legs. As her small, strong hands worked over him, a drunken smile quivered across Gáu-Gung's face, and he began to pant feebly with his big gray tongue hanging out like the paper from a spent firecracker. I can't do this forever.

Neither can he, Jessica said, stroking Puppy-pa's white face. If you don't take care of this now, you're just leaving your problems to me.

Jessica's mom continued to rub the concoction on Gáu-Gung's back legs, tail and anus, her dark eyes as focused and piercing as arrowheads. Not problems, she grunted, still working. What I'm leaving you is life.

A THOUSAND COUNTED AND UNREPENTANT DEBTS

Bill stirred the ice in his rum and cola with a finger. "Listen, I'm a connoisseur of bad decisions. My philosophy is to make every decision based on what's most interesting—and sex work is definitely interesting."

Reneia was bouncing Pryce, Bill's daughter, on her knee, singing "Ride a Little Pony" as the baby gnawed on an apple. Between verses, she commented breathlessly: "I never set out to become a lady—*down to town!*—but I never thought I'd end up in so much debt."

We all could be free if we stopped counting, Bill thought; he said, "*Whoopsie, whoopsie*—for twenty dollars… *I'll… go…down!*"

"People do far worse for far less. At least I'm not middle management."

Bill nodded. "And you'd be popular."

"Popular?"

"Nowadays the girls with scarlet letters are the popular ones."

Reneia grinned, devilishly. "I'm the type of girl who writes her name in scarlet letters."

They were sitting in the kitchen of his apartment. It was a small, outdated room with faded brown cabinets, a black electric oven, and white linoleum flooring.

Whenever the wind blew, a suffocating wave of hot evening air would wail through the small window above the sink and rattle the plastic table. "You're a life coach," Reneia said. "Give me your professional opinion. No Socratic questions allowed."

Bill took a drink; the sweetness of the rum was a refreshing reprieve from the heat. He said, "I think you'll incur another type of debt."

"Is there another type?"

He reached out and tickled the folds of fat beneath his daughter's chin. "If you pay off your financial debt this way I think you'll incur debt that's harder to pay off—emotional debt."

"Emotional debt, eh?"

"Emotional, psychological—you get the idea."

Pryce lunged for Bill, and he took over the reins of bouncing her down to town. It was starting to get dark; the splendor of shadows poured into the room and left the hard-living doppelgangers of their glasses gray on the table. The white noise of the traffic on the freeway began to fade, and the subdued lights of Los Angeles in the distance twinkled like stars caught in a dense smog. Balancing Pryce deftly on one hip, Bill made another round of drinks and replaced Pryce's apple with an ice cube.

Reneia reached out absently and tapped his hand with a boney finger. "Ten grand," she said, gazing into her drink as if it were a memory. "That's why I'm *going* to do it."

"Ten grand—so what? The whole country is in debt."

"That's a lot of debt! And it only grows, never expires!"

"It sounds like this goes deeper than debt slavery."

"Either I sell my body or rob a bank, and I figure selling my body is less dangerous."

"Debt may not expire, but people do. It could be more dangerous."

"I'm not going to be on the corner. The booker will keep the website running and take the calls. All I'll be doing is waiting for guys to come to the motel room."

Bill grinned. "Sounds like your typical Tuesday night."

Reneia smiled, a glow like a lunar eclipse passing over her face. Bill stared at her for a moment. Sitting perfectly still, Reneia had the aspect of a statue of a nymph rooted in deep contemplation. Her dusk skin was smooth and radiant beneath the luxurious whirls of night raining down upon her shoulders. The mounds of her cheeks were well-defined and regal, alluding to a life of luxury she had never known, and her lips were full and sensual, swollen with the momentary affections of countless men she had loved countless times, if only for a perilous string of surrenders. She was the most captivating thing he had ever seen, and it made him feel utterly powerless. He said, "Sometimes your hair reminds me of a nun's hood."

She guffawed—a blurt of exultation that triggered an exaggerated, slow-motion slap of her knee. She bit her lip, playfully. "A nun's hood—now there's next year's Halloween costume."

Half past a bottle of rum: it was time to put the baby to bed. Bill carried Pryce into her bedroom where fanciful *Winnie the Pooh* characters decorated the walls, and stuffed animals loitered upon every surface. He laid her down, turned her mobile on, and marveled at her bright face aglow with curiosity as flutey tones floated into the darkness. As she suckled her bottle, she looked up at him with her upturned eyes crystalline in the dark; then, with a flutter of eyelashes, she fell asleep.

Back in the kitchen, Bill and Reneia ate bologna sandwiches and potato chips out of idle desperation. As they sat eating, Bill tried to justify to himself why he was worthy of being a father. He knew that the day was approaching when pain and fear would mark the way Pryce saw herself, and he knew there was nothing he could do to erase the distortion. She would be on her own. In a real way, she already was.

"I don't know," Reneia said, the spider legs of her fingers walking the web of her earlobe. "I just want to start fresh. It's not like I'd be killing someone. If I can't find The One to love me for the rest of my life, then I want men to pay to love me for a moment."

"We only love sets of circumstances," Bill opined, following the cascade of her black hair down to her shoulder, thinking very much that these circumstances were one of those sets.

An empty bottle later, they were in bed staring away from each other in the dark. He could feel the warmth of Reneia's body exactly too far away to be comforting. *I don't want you to do it,* he thought; he closed his eyes and spent a sleepless night in silence.

†

"We should go to Vegas," Bill said.

They were sitting in the living room, the coffee table between them like an empty casket. Modeling atop it were two empty bottles of pinot grigio.

"We should," Reneia said, curling her hair into a succession of black dollar signs around her finger.

"Pryce is with her mom for the weekend, so we could drive out and gamble all night, then get a room for tomorrow night."

"Let's go."

They started a new bottle, this one a chardonnay that tasted like moldy oak and honey. Neither of them moved.

"So I have to tell you about last night," Reneia said, packing sticky leaves of marijuana into a glass pipe. Taking a long drag, she blew out a thick plume of smoke. "The Diplomat was patronized," she croaked. "Tequila and beer were consumed, and some good ole fashioned heavy petting ensued. Customers complained, and rather rude orders to exit the bar were given."

"I see you're prepared for your career as a politician."

"But get this—while we're driving back to the apartment he's crashing at, he wants me to blow him. I ask, 'what if we get in an accident and I die with a dick in my mouth?' And this asshole has the gall to say, 'Then you'll die as you lived.'"

"Ouch!"

"I punch him, and he has the nerve to call me emotional and erratic! It's another goddamn case of paralysis by abundance—there's too much sex in L.A."

"I love your erratic behavior," Bill said, his face turning red as he struggled to hold in a cloud of smoke.

"I'm telling you, Bill—it's impossible to find a real man nowadays. They're all just insecure, inadequate *boys*." Reneia's eyes fogged over, shrouded by a city full of seedy alleys and broken homes. Within her gaze a thousand sins, counted and unrepentant, grew as thick and suffocating as smog. "So I'm not going to do the call girl thing," she said, taking a swig of chardonnay. "Maybe I'll look into modeling. Or acting. Maybe I'll join a band. Or I'll move to Utah with Christine and become a Mormon."

He listened, her words giving birth to more and more options, all of which seemed possible but years and miles away. She regarded him with a look he couldn't discern. It was as if she had been descrying him from a distance and as she stared he came swiftly into view; or was it a look of him disappearing into the distance? Hello and goodbye; they were both in her eyes. And a quiet but throbbing part of him wanted to know them both. "You know there will be someone with you no matter how many times you reinvent yourself."

"Don't give me your life coaching crap," she said. "I grew up a Jehovah's Witness. After you've witnessed God, there's no way you can believe in Him."

Reneia's cell phone rang—"I'm Every Woman" by Whitney Houston. After a brief conversation, they were on their way to meet some friends at Beauty Bar in Hollywood. They drove up the 118 freeway that tears like an open wound through the San Fernando Valley to the 405 with its thin lanes and constant merging above the valley. They merged onto the 101 freeway and stopped behind a herd of red lights. After twenty minutes of stop-and-little-go traffic, they veered onto the Sunset Boulevard exit, past the KTLA television studio, and parked at a meter a couple of blocks from the bar. Making their way to the bar, they stopped briefly to admire the Christmas tree aglow atop the Capitol Records building, the heat of the night smoldering in mocking contempt of the season.

"It's beginning to look a lot like Christmas."

Reneia adjusted her bra while examining her breasts in the side mirror of a parked car. "Maybe it will snow in the bar."

"I love you."

"I know. And you know you're the only man for me."

Beauty Bar was a long, narrow building separated into two sections. The first section had a bar that ran lengthwise along the right wall, a disc jockey booth near the opening to the second section, and a row of scoop-shaped chairs opposite the bar. The back section consisted of vinyl couches with counters along the walls. It was fifteen minutes past ten, so it was still too early to be crowded, and Reneia and Bill were able to order a couple of vodka tonics and make their way to the back without any impromptu games of standing Twister.

In the back, a standard assembly of drinking acquaintances was clumped together on a couch; Bill had never bothered to remember most of their names. Reneia took a seat and sat with her legs crossed and her drink on her knee—the ice like melting diamonds in her glass. Tall and broad-shouldered, Bill stood before them like a ghost hell-bent on ensuring the past is never forgotten, his sharp features outlined by throbbing bursts of neon light. He raised his glass: "A toast—to the end of Prohibition!"

The group responded with enthusiastic wassails then quickly dispersed throughout the bar. Reneia began dancing with a nefarious character bearing an uncanny resemblance to Frankenstein, and Bill took a seat at the bar. Ordering an old fashioned, he very much wished they had gone to Vegas.

"All well?" Reneia asked a few minutes later; apparently, the guy she had been dancing with had important calls to make, so he was outside flailing his hands spastically. Bill couldn't help but imagine Frankenstein calling his wife—*no, honey, it's not what you think. I didn't mean to miss your birthday dinner—I was dead!*

"All's good"—he popped the maraschino cherry from his old fashioned into his mouth—"So I take it the wolfman was busy tonight."

Reneia laughed. "Barkeep—the next round's on my pimp!" With a flutter of her fingers, she laid the blue rectangle of her credit card down on the silver metal bar. "So I'm going to do it."

"Do what?"

Blowing a stray strand of hair from her face, she said, "You know—the *massages*."

"Oh. When did that change?"

"Just a few minutes ago. The booker called. I start on Tuesday."

"Seems like a sensible day to start."

She slapped the credit card. "Two hundred and fifty dollars an hour, Bill! For *one* hour. I can pay off my debt in a work week."

"It's better than working pro bono with the Frankensteins of the world."

"It really is charity. Definitely not love at first slice. I don't know what my subconscious could be thinking."

Examining the glass tips of the bottles of liquor, Bill asked, "You sure you want to do this?"

"He's not much to look at, but he's super creative. He showed me a sketch he made of Noah's Ark floating on a sea of fire, and Noah's releasing a trout instead of a dove."

I wasn't talking about Frankenstein, Bill thought; he asked, "What's the Ark made of?"

"Wrought iron, I think."

Bill scoffed—"Creativity without intelligence is just newness."

"Whatever that's supposed to mean," Reneia dismissed. "It looks like Franky's off the phone. I'm going to take off."

Bill explored his glass. "Are you sure you can trust him?"

"Franky? Why not? I'm not planning on playing hard to get."

"Because he thinks he's clever."

"You think you're clever."

"And I'm not a man of my word; I'm a man of words, none of which I'm particularly committed to. Who could trust a guy like that?"

She smiled, a whirl of playfulness, disillusion, and longing. Hugging Bill, she pulled just far enough away that he could taste the cannabis and vodka on her breath. The corners of their lips touched as she whispered: "The real question is—are we bad people who sometimes do good things, or good people who do bad things? Trust is irrelevant."

Bill turned back to the bar, dipped his finger into his old fashioned, and began to swirl the large sphere of ice. The smell of Reneia's hair lingered in his nose, and his skin tingled from the caress of her lips against his cheek. He had meant Tuesday—*are you sure you want to go through with Tuesday?* And he had meant that he would be there no matter how many times she reinvented herself, not some god.

"You're spilling," the bartender told him.

He hadn't realized he'd begun stirring so rigorously. He held up a dripping digit. "To Tuesday," he said, and sucked the bourbon off his finger.

†

"You know what my problem is? It's that I love too hard."

Bill looked at her placidly. Amanda James had come in for a life coaching session on how to better manage her life to get ahead at work. Bill had yet to hear about where she worked or what she did for a living, but he had heard about Erik, her dickhead ex, and her coffee drink of choice, a Grande Extra Shot Soy Upside Down White Mocha Latte. He asked, "What strategies do you think you can take to love less hard?"

"What the fuck does that have to do with work?" she asked.

Bill continued to look at her placidly. During his eighty-hour onboarding training, Bill had been taught to allow, even encourage, clients to ramble off on tangents. It was supposed to make the client feel better about spending their money, and, most importantly, result in more billable hours to reach "resolution." Bill found this last part especially amusing: he wasn't sure he'd ever approached anything resembling a resolution. He asked, "Do you think loving too hard is slowing your career growth?"

She took a sip of her Grande Extra Shot Soy Upside Down White Mocha Latte. "The thing is, loving too hard is *enhancing* my career. What's holding me back is climate change. It's so hot I'm forced to show all this skin, and it's too distracting for my poor boss. What I really need is cardigan weather."

He took a deep breath and doodled on his notepad. This client's particular brand of ripping topics from the headlines to fuse with her narcissism was proving to be too irritating for him to suffer quietly. Worse, her obnoxious choice of beverage and habit of "loving too hard" reminded him of Catherine, Pryce's mom. His mind wandered to a time when he and Catherine were still together and he was still delusional enough to believe he could make a living writing fiction. He was sitting on his bed, writing some piece of garbage about a boy with arrested development aimlessly stalking his mother's killer for decades, when Catherine walked in wearing a sheer negligee...

"I want to have a baby," Amanda James said presently, turning her heart-shaped face like a praying mantis inspecting a potential mate. "But I don't know what I'd say to my child about the border wall..."

Bill looked at his client dumbly, just as dumbly as he had looked at Catherine when she broached the subject with him. In both cases, he just kept writing and didn't respond. At the time, he had been debating proposing to Catherine for months. He kept considering the adage, *a writer makes decisions*, but there were too many possibilities to think anything was possible, so he let his inactivity decide for him. He never asked. He remembered the way the heat felt radiating from Catherine's body as she straddled him, the rustle of his paper as he set his writing down. And he remembered thinking that they should talk about it, give the decision some time. But then the decision flooded out of him, and in a surge of exultation, Catherine triumphantly pressed him deeper into her.

"Are you listening to me?" Amanda James asked. "I think that last piece about police brutality and the glass ceiling was important. You're a white male—*give me the code.*"

He looked at her, less than placidly. "What day of the week is it?" he asked, more coldly than intended.

"Tuesday," she answered, mystified by the question.

"Always work on Tuesdays. White men hate it when you take Tuesdays off."

"Oh, that's good!" she moaned, working her thumbs hurriedly over the touchscreen of her phone. Taking an enthusiastic gulp of her half-full Grande Extra Shot Soy Upside Down White Mocha Latte, she asked, "What about half days?"

Bill gritted his teeth—"Just work the whole day."

"This is going to be rough, but this is good—it's good. I can do this!"

He wrote *Tuesday* on his notepad. He thought about calling Reneia but knew he wouldn't. What was he going to say? Break a leg? Again he was reminded of the quote—*a writer makes decisions.* Shifting uncomfortably in his chair, Bill remembered applying to Cast the New You, LLC the afternoon after first hearing Pryce's heartbeat, leaving behind any silly notion of becoming an author. On the margin of his notepad, he wrote: *Are there any writers still alive today?*

"You know," Amanda James said, looking up from her phone with an expression like she'd just seen God's face in a brushfire. "I think my real problem is that I don't love *myself* hard enough."

Don't say it, Bill thought; he seethed, "If you loved yourself at all, you'd kill yourself."

Amanda James looked at him with the frozen smile of a person who doesn't get the joke but is certain one has just been told.

"The front desk can take your payment," Bill said, setting his notepad down. "Debit is preferred, but I'm sure you'll be paying with credit."

Amanda James's eyes bulged out of their sockets. Then she smiled, and it was so genuine that for a second Bill thought he'd finally witnessed resolution. The next moment she slapped him across the face with her half-empty Grande Extra Shot Soy Upside Down White Mocha Latte. "You're a piece of shit," she hissed, pressing a high heel into his crotch. "There's no way anyone could ever love you. If it took me twenty minutes to figure that out, it won't take anyone else long."

With Amanda James's heel digging into his groin and sickly sweet foam dripping down his face and into his ear, Bill suddenly felt a swelling of admiration for her. "Good for you," he said. "Now take that attitude to work next Tuesday."

†

She had stripped the bedspread (because bedspreads in hotels are vile) and the fuzzy duvet cover (because they always made her feel like she was rolling in sand) off the bed and was lying on the sheet in her bra and panties. Her bra and panties were black, and she liked the way her bronze skin looked against the white of the sheets and the way the half-empty bottle of Southern Comfort with its red lettering looked between her thighs. She could hear footsteps marching down the walkway. They reminded her of the sound of her father's footsteps pacing down the hallway when she was seventeen, coming to tell her she had been disfellowshipped from the church for touching Adam Grossman's penis. Touching a penis outside of the sanctity of marriage is a sin, he had said in his measured English that only made the South African accent he was trying to hide all the more pronounced. Then the memory of her father's voice was muddied by muffled voices in the next room. The door squealed open. The Southern Comfort rushed to her lips, leaving a dry, sweet taste on her tongue. The stranger sat down on the edge of the bed and unbuckled his pants. Reneia could smell the musty, woody notes of the oud in his cologne—thick and suffocating like the smell of gas. She heard the intercourse between his whiny mutterings and her breathy whispers, but couldn't understand any of the words. Before she could take another swig, he was upon her, inside her, and grunting. The Southern Comfort fell off the bed and hit the floor with a sound like a door shutting. The slapping of their bodies colliding sounded like the footfalls of disfellowship. Disfellowship from God, the church, her dad, her family, her history, society and all respectability. Sweat dripped from his chest onto her face, and the weight of his belly left her breathless each time he thrust. Reneia gritted her teeth and counted every grunt—calculating precisely how much each paid.

†

The phone rang.

"I'm coming over."

"What's wrong?"

"I did it."

What time was it? The baby?—still asleep. Bill took a slug of whiskey, set the bottle back down on the nightstand.

"You did it?"

"Yes. Are you going to get me off? I need to get off."

Reneia's voice was manic, hysterical. Bill tried to think through the fog of sleep, drunkenness, and confusion. He considered throwing a robe or some pajamas on, but remembered he didn't own either. He took another swallow of whiskey and asked, "Where are you?"

"I'm on my way over. I did it, Bill. I did *it*."

Finally, it occurred to him what she had done, and he realized he had known all along—it was Tuesday.

"I'm pulling up. Meet me outside."

He carefully picked Pryce up and cradled her limp body in his arms, the glow from the nightlight wrapping a golden aura around her head. He took her to her room and laid her in her crib, then hustled down the cement stairs to the parking lot.

"Funny meeting you here," Bill said as he opened the door of her car. His heart was beating so violently it made his knees shake.

Reneia was wearing a flowered sundress. Her breasts were lathered in sweat, and an open can of Bud Light was stuffed between her thighs.

"What the fuck took you so long?" she slurred, fumbling with the seatbelt.

"Traffic."

She attempted to take a drink, coughed, and spit a mouthful of beer down her dress. Tossing the can at his crotch, she looked up at him with bloodshot eyes. "I want you to fuck me. Do whatever you want. I just want to hear you say my name."

He trembled. The fog rescinded and there was only Reneia—her breasts, her lips, her hands. If these were the circumstances, he would take them—take her. "Get out of the car, Reneia."

She slid out of the car and pulled him by the waist of his underwear up the stairs and into the bedroom. Stopping at the foot of the bed, she faced him, bit her lip, and slapped him across the face.

"*Reneia*"—he quivered, lip swelling—"take off your fucking dress."

With her eyes locked on his, she slipped the dress off over her head. Completely naked, she swept a hurricane of hair off her shoulders.

He reached for her.

She slapped his hand.

He reached again.

She belted him across the face.

Stepping to him, she dug her nails into his chest and clawed straight down to his waist. Beads of blood formed a dotted trail to his navel. Without looking away from him, she sat down on the corner of the bed and crossed her legs.

Grabbing her knees, Bill tried to pry her legs apart, but she rebuked him. They locked eyes. Clenching his jaw, he forced her legs open. A devilish smile spread across her face—she reached into the nightstand and withdrew a condom.

"Say it," she insisted.

He almost whimpered—"Reneia…"

She flung the condom to the floor, spit on her hand, and guided him inside.

"Reneia," he moaned into her cheek. "Reneia!"

"Choke me," she panted, wrapping her legs around his hips.

He did as told, transforming her moans into soundless cries. After a few thrusts, he released his grip.

She gasped. Took a desperate breath. Then implored: "Keep choking me. Don't stop. You're going to make me come."

He wrapped his hand around her throat. She dug her fingernails into his chest, digging until his grip tightened. "Say it," she eked out.

"Reneia," he groaned, squeezing and thrusting with all his might. "Reneia, Reneia, Reneia—*Reneia!*"

He rolled off of her, wheezing. Every thought distorted and twisted into another. His body ached for her; the realization that he hadn't worn a condom filled him with panic; what was this going to mean tomorrow?—now that he'd had her there was no going back.

He sat up and placed his hands behind his head. He dared a glance at Reneia, just enough to see that she hadn't moved.

Did she hate him? Was he just another John? Did he get too excited and finish before he got the job done?

He looked back again.

She still hadn't moved.

Terror shot down his chest, wrapping around his heart and sizzling the length of every nerve and vein like a cold burn. The air froze in his lungs. Weakly, he reached out and pressed a trembling finger to her hip. No response.

"Reneia?"

He fumbled for her wrist, desperate for a grunt, a flinch, a pulse.

Nothing.

Bill sprang to his feet and backpedaled across the room, crashing into the dresser so hard it sent him flailing to the floor. His head bashed against the corner of the bed. Blood streamed down his face. Scampering to his feet, he fell again, slamming his shoulder into the ground. He clawed up the dresser, looked back at Reneia, and felt frantically for his car keys. As he took the keys in his hand, he trembled so violently he couldn't breathe. He took a step for the door. Then he heard Pryce stir in the next room, and hesitated.

AMEN

PEOPLE ALWAYS REMEMBER the miracle of wine," Mother Tiffany says with a grave shake of the head, "but they forget the hellacious hangover the morning after." And with that, Mother Tiffany concludes her sermon on the importance of being careful what you pray for, thanks Me for My blessings, and reminds everyone for the sixty-seventh time—"Poopé Hal will be making his campaign stop at this evening's Sunset Mass, so wear your good underwear, people!"

Behind Mother Tiffany, adorned in an aqua robe with a flamboyant pink collar, Mary Fields kneels in the choir with a galloping heart. Although she isn't sure if she thinks Poopé Hal or his competitor, Father Donald, is cuter, she is giddy that the most powerful man in the nation will be hearing her sing in less than thirteen hours. As Mother Tiffany exits the stage, the choir rises and begins to sing My praises:

> *Our Liege gives us choices*
> *A million paths to faith*
> *And when life leaves us*
> *We'll have our final vote to make*
> *Our vote will redeem us*
> *Or cast us upon The Waves —*

So if you want to sing with Evian's notes
Just be true to our Liege and cast your vote—
Give Mother your time and Father your rhyme
And don't slow traffic—because it's a crime!

With Mary's atonal howling drowning out the rest of the choir, Father John slips into the confessional, hoping that Mary will develop laryngitis before sunset. But knowing that Mary will sing even if her throat prunes into a pillar of salt, he is left praying he will die a heroic death and be rewarded by seventy-six *mute* lovers of dubious backgrounds. Father John thinks, *an eternity with only the sweet music of leather chaps clapping?—now* that *would be divine!*

Bobby Johnson, who often falls asleep during The Good Trilogy study, slinks into Father John's confessional with credit card in hand. After kissing the feet of a statue of My nephew Gump, the patron saint of travel, Bobby readies himself to pay for his sins. First, he confesses to telling thirteen white lies and one flaming red one (*This is the first time this has ever happened, seriously!*). Father John stabs the numbers into the accounting calculator, and it cackles as it prints out the receipt: one dollar a white lie—$13.00—and for the flaming red one—$7.50. Bobby then admits to not holding the door open for an elderly lady—$6.60—to not telling his mom her new haircut made her face look fat—$6.00—and to slowing down to gawk at a car accident on the other side of the freeway—$26.66. Typically an honest taxpayer, Bobby does leave out the thirty-one animals he slaughtered in a game he calls "Drive Over Buffet." Though it says in The Good Trilogy, "Thou shalt not senselessly disembowel, dismember, mutilate or sodomize thy animal colleagues," Bobby had long ago concluded that this passage was just filler, and as a result, he doesn't believe he should pay sin tax for this indulgence. But there is one deed he's committed that he's sure is wicked, and the guilt of this memory itches as incessantly as an embarrassing rash...

Bobby takes a deep breath. Racing his eyes in their sockets, Father John sighs—he knows exactly what Bobby is going to say: "I also want to pay for touching Suzy Masterson's breasts before my Of Age party."

$3.50

Even though Bobby recently held his Of Age party during his sixteenth birthday and thus is encouraged to go forth and procreate, he still prays at least once a day, begging Me to forgive him for touching Suzy's breasts on his *fourteenth* birthday. Adding to his shame is the ever-present chiding of his mother who routinely warns him that if he doesn't change his indifferent ways, he'll suffer the same fate as his bastardly uncle who never allowed cars to merge in front of him. Bobby becomes especially self-conscious of this vile possibility whenever Poopé Hal makes a fundraising visit leading up to an election.

This year's election became especially hallowed on April first, My birthday, when I heard Poopé candidate Donald plotting to reduce highway construction if elected. I realize now My error in not being more precise about the sanctity of travel. Travel is one of the three sacred acts. Why else would I have had My people wander the deserts and mountains and prairies and coasts for seventy-three years, seven months and thirteen days? But due to bad grammar and creative differences with My grandson when he was writing My word, people take travel for granted. I mean, do they really think I want them spending their days sitting on the couch saying "amen" to *Oprah* while taking pictures of their tacos and "liking" mugshots on the internet? I spent six years creating their home, and I want them to travel it, to witness the wonders of My architecture, to enjoy the road I hoed. But alas, *Oprah* is one hell of an entertainer, and the seduction of Selfie Wednesday often leads My followers to the blasphemous pastures of apathy. And now the possible leader of My nation—My potential public relations man!—is hellbent on *reducing* road construction and leaving millions of people stranded in the purgatory of rush hour traffic. So although it has been forty-three years since I last meddled in politics, I find myself doing so now.

Father John finishes with the remaining confessors and begins to add up the sin tax collection. The amount is staggering compared to a normal Monday, but for a Poopé's visit, it is typical. John writes $74,352.13 into the logbook, conveniently forgetting to add the thirty-six dollars he slips into his pocket, CEO-like. Theft is a vile act, but John intends to take a cruise pilgrimage for the holy month of floods, the celebration commemorating the time I covered the world in water to encourage boat travel. Seeing as it is for a noble and righteous end, and it isn't habitual, I allow him to steal just enough to fulfill his appetite.

"Father John," Mother Tiffany says as she peeks into the confessional. "Are you ready? We need to meet Poopé Hal at the train station."

Immediately the fantasy of ripping Mother Tiffany into the sin tax booth ignites in Father John's mind. There is banging. An awkward high five. The confessional walls shudder. The calculator chatters. And it concludes with him leaving her a bill accounting for each thrust, tip included.

"Father John, 'the quicker the tongue, the faster the passengers come aboard,'" Mother Tiffany says, irritated by both her silk Priestess collar and Father John's slow wit. She is using the quote out of context, though. The true meaning is always to be quick to answer questions when going through customs so you don't hold up the line.

Father John follows Mother Tiffany out of the confessional, his heart beating with the sound of leather clapping like approaching thunder.

✝

Father John greets Poopé Hal with a rigid bow, thinking that at five foot four inches, Hal is tall for a Poopé. Quietly fiddling with his harmonica, Poopé Hal lumbers into the backseat of the limousine. His disciples, who are all at least two inches shorter than Hal, scurry into the limo after him. All the disciples have bald heads and wear silk robes that resemble oversized pink togas. Father John thinks: *their outfits are super cute!* Climbing into the limousine last, Mother Tiffany barks at the chauffeur: "Make it fast, driver. Back to the temple. 'Let not the minutes bury you, on— *on!*—travel for the great man.'"

Staying faithful to her ignorance, Mother Tiffany misquoted the passage. It actually reads: "Let not the minutes bury you in traffic, go—*go*—travel is *great*, man!"

"Mother Tiffany," Poopé Hal says as he strokes her knee with the harmonica, "Please sit in the front with the biohazard. I require privacy."

Indignant and confused over the Poopé's dismissal and feeling very much as if she'd just been dumped again, Mother Tiffany nods and says: "Let's go, Father John. The Poopé desires his sacred privacy. 'Listen to the wind, heed the wind, break wind.'"

That's not even remotely in The Good Trilogy.

"No. I've been commanded to speak with Father John. *Alone.*"

He wasn't lying. I really had commanded him to speak with Father John.

Mother Tiffany exits with a huff—a limp collapse and thirty spastic kicks from a full-fledged temper tantrum. Taking a voracious breath, she consoles herself with the fact that at least she wouldn't have to feel the Poopé's raw-hide-textured fingers scraping against her silk, *although* she did like the smooth, metallic feel of his harmonica as it slid up her inner thigh… *No! Damn it—I hate men,* Mother Tiffany thinks. *Screw this. I'm going to take a cab. I'm not going to fall for another cold, oversexed jerk wielding a big stick. 'Blessed is the staff used with prudence.' I pray the Poopé finds his holiness.*

She actually got that one right, but I was referring to a different staff.

After Mother Tiffany slams the door, the Poopé says, "Father John, I know about your feelings for Mother Tiffany, and about your fantasy of ravaging her—*sexually*—in the confessional. And I also know about the extra cash you skim from the sin tax collection."

Father John sits quietly, his eyes splashing back and forth in their sockets. Suddenly, he lusts for a drink.

†

The last few moments before Poopé Hal takes the stage are filled with the guttural groaning of Mary's warm-up routine accompanied by thirteen frantic prayers for a plague of deafness. I can't answer them, though, because Mary's a swing vote and the Poopé and I need every vote we can get. Perhaps crooning for the Poopé will get her vote, but I can never be entirely sure. If it comes down to it, I will have Poopé Hal remind her that I know she dropped My birthday goat on the floor and then fed it to Mother Tiffany and Father John, a deceit she has never paid her tax for.

As Poopé Hal steps behind the podium, a long, crooked grin spreads across his face. His presence immediately quiets the mouths of the congregation as they show reverence with their silence; although their physical, emotional and mental chaos roars, sinfully. Upon seeing Poopé Hal, Father John hoists a glass of sacramental wine to his lips and begins to suckle. Taking one look at the Poopé's hands gripping the podium, Mary's heart boils with exhilaration. She prays: *Mother and Father, may my singing arouse such emotion in Poopé Hal that he's inspired to join me!* The Poopé's exuberance and power cause Bobby to recoil, wishing as he shrinks into his seat that he'd paid twice for touching Suzy's breasts.

"With the trials our nation faces," begins the Poopé, "now, more than ever before, we need *experienced* leadership, comfortable walking shoes, and *more* roads."

Mother Tiffany enters the temple, her auburn hair askew and her thick makeup smudged and wet. During the cab ride, she'd decided two things: she's *not* going to vote for Poopé Hal, and she is going to pour her grandmother's ashes onto a mirror, cut them into neat gray lines, and snort them like cocaine when she gets home.

With a wave of his palm, Poopé Hal motions for a disciple to bring him the Ark of the Toilette. A disciple hurries a rectangular object covered by a black shroud across the stage.

Cringing, Bobby pleads to Me: *please let it be a hamster under that veil.*

"Repent now," the Poopé roars with theatrical rage. "Before you too are like"—he whips the shroud off of the Ark of the Toilette, revealing a village of dung beetles and a fresh cow pie. "Look at the little devils!" the Poopé giggles with a sadistic grin. "Repent now before you too spend eternity rolling balls of *poop!*"

Bobby thinks: *Suzy's A-cups were so not worth being reincarnated into a dung beetle.*

Father John—who only drank the sip of sacramental wine handed out each week at Sunset Mass, nothing more—refills his glass.

The dung beetles toil away in their glass dungeon, their black eyes oblivious and their six legs working in single-minded devotion. Above them in pink neon reads: "Hell, You Better Believe."

†

Once the Poopé finishes his sermon, I command him to campaign to Bobby. As he is exiting the stage, the choir's voice rises in song and the somewhat sweet, completely screeching quality of their tone bellows out:

Our vote will redeem us
Or cast us upon the waves —

Bobby's leg becomes wet and warm as Poopé Hal sits down next to him. "Graces," Bobby says, shaking. Trying to regain his always-fragile poise, Bobby thinks: *I have nothing to be ashamed of. I paid. Good money. More than once!*

Father John, sitting in the pew directly behind Bobby and Poopé Hal, begins guzzling from the teat of the bottle. With a curiosity begat from an apocalyptic sense of humor, Father John lurches forward to spy on Bobby and the Poopé's conversation.

"Bobby, I've been commanded to speak with you." After a dramatic pause, Poopé Hal says: "Son, I know about the evil of your hands on your fourteenth birthday."

"My... my *fourteenth* birthday? What'd I do on my *fourteenth* birthday?"

"You touched Suzy Masterson's breasts. Do not forget that you are *always* being watched. Our Liege is Mother and Father and Big Brother."

"I touched Suzy's boobs—I mean... *hooters. No*— breasts! On my *fifteenth* birthday."

The Poopé sits quietly, momentarily confounded; his face ripens as if a lover has just caught him popping a handful of Viagra.

Father John takes a swig directly from the bottle of wine.

"How did you know that I touched Suzy's, well, you know?"

"I was told by Big Brother."

"Then how come you got the birthday wrong?"

Father John reaches under the pew and grabs another bottle.

†

As Mary begins her solo, she searches for the Poopé among the congregation. Crooning so loudly it drowns out all the feral cats in the neighborhood, her eyes cast upon the Poopé. He is talking with Mother Tiffany and completely ignoring her singing. Blood rushes to her cheeks as fury fills her lungs:

Give Mother your time and Father your rhyme
And don't slow traffic—because it's a crime!

Poopé Hal grabs Mother Tiffany's hand and whispers: "I know what you intend to do with your grandmother's ashes when you return home tonight."

"What are you talking about?" Mother Tiffany asks, trying not to sound insolent. Pulling her hand out from beneath the Poopé's, she scratches her nose to make the act seem like an obligation to biology and not an act of repulsion.

Father John watches them, drinking, grinning in a mixture of mischievous delight and impending horror. As Mary's voice scrapes metallically over a high note, John winces and places his hands over his burning eardrums. When he pulls his hands away, his palms are red with his blood.

"You plan to snort her ashes like some drug, for a high."

The Poopé's words pierce Mother Tiffany. She thinks: "the words of the wise often sound like nonsense to the ears of the humble." She tries to decipher the intent of the parable the Poopé told her, but she can divine no meaning. Poopé Hal is being quite literal, though, and The Good Trilogy actually reads: "the words of kings and judges are often nonsensical to the ears of the truly wise, the humble."

Mary concludes her solo with a sinful screeching of My name. Swishing back and forth in his seat, Father John claps like an otter that's just escaped captivity and discovered that a bucket of fish is greeting him at the beach.

Poopé Hal says, "Mother Tiffany, 'the toll of secrecy is a recurring charge that becomes quite expensive when you travel the road daily'"—he completely made that up, but I kind of like it—"If you want me to turn a blind eye as you snort Grandma, then I'll need your vote of confidence."

"Are you feeling okay, Poopé Hal? My grandmother is still alive."

†

Poopé Hal and I spend fifteen minutes talking in a confessional following evening mass. After he moans and whines, asking Me why I have forsaken him, I command him to stay on script and to seek out Mary. Although I must confess to a bit of confusion—because I'd swear Bobby touched Suzy's breasts on his *fourteenth* birthday and not on his *fifteenth* as he claimed, and I thought I'd greeted Tiffany's grandmother at the gate Myself—I'm sure there is a simple reason for these mishaps that I'm overlooking due to my preoccupation with the Poopé race. Perhaps I am getting people confused; maybe it was Mother Bambi, the backup Mother, who plans on snorting her grandma's ashes. Maybe I have events mixed up: maybe Bobby did something else he is ashamed of on his fourteenth birthday, something sinful and sordid, like leaving debris in the road... Or perhaps it isn't Me at all! Maybe Mother Tiffany and Father John and Bobby are just—are just—*crazy people!*

Poopé Hal finds Mary kneeling next to a brass statue of my obese niece, Rosy (the archangel of feasts). His disciples follow him, dutifully, and John drinks, gluttonously, now on his third bottle.

"Why the tears?" Poopé Hal asks as he sits down Indian-style next to Mary.

"Thank you for asking, but I don't think that you really care."

"Why wouldn't I care, my dear?"

He is really cute, Mary thinks. "I saw you talking to Mother Tiffany. I don't think you even heard me sing."

"Your music means a great deal to you."

"Oh, yes. It means everything to me. After Mother and Father, of course."

Poopé Hal pulls out his harmonica and slides it from her knee up her inner thigh: "Everyone thinks it's silly, but it's my *second* passion."

"You're a musician!"

"Yes, with only the reward of self-gratification."

Poopé Hal puts his hand on her hip. She takes his hand in hers. "I may be an older ride," the Poopé whispers huskily into her ear, "but I still have enough gas in the tank for short trips." Mary leads Poopé Hal into the confessional, and they clumsily pull each other's clothes off. Normally I wouldn't approve of casual sex inside of a confessional, but under the circumstances it was divine.

After Poopé Hal finishes securing Mary's vote, he exits the confessional. He is greeted by the flamboyant curtsies of the disciples who had sat outside the confessional during the campaign. The disciples follow Hal to the green room where he tells Tiffany that he has been ordered by Me to give a midnight sermon. Hal then prays with his disciples for divine intervention. Things are desperate. If Poopé Hal doesn't win this temple he'll surely lose the election and the already crowded freeways and highways will only become more of a perpetual funeral precession. I have to concentrate and pay particular attention to detail.

†

When the Poopé is out of sight, Mother Tiffany and Father John move swiftly to Mary, who sits smoking in the confessional.

"Mary, are you in there?" Mother Tiffany calls.

Mary, glistening in a raincoat of sweat, puts her cigarette out on the statue of Gump and steps out of the confessional.

"Mary, were ya just—*communing*—wit' dah Poopé?" Father John slurs, wobbling like a drunken sailor during a hurricane.

"Oh, was I ever," Mary gushes. "And it was *good*."

"Did he say anything *strange* to you," Mother Tiffany asks, doing her best to ignore Father John's drunken stupor.

"No. But he sure got my vote."

"Mary, Poopé Hal is a *sick* puppy-dog. We gotta nose *exactly* wa he toe'd ya."

"How dare you! My words *and* actions with the Poopé are none of your business. I would expect more from you two, I sure would. And you could use a mint *and* a shower in the worst way, Father John."

"Did the Poopé say he was on a mission, a mission from Mother and Father? Did he claim to know intimate details about your life?"

"No. Thank you, but I'll be leaving now." Mary exits to find the Poopé.

"We have to do something. 'Those who remain idle in the den of sin shall inherit sin,'" Mother Tiffany says as she looks into Father John's blood-striped eyes and watches him sway back and forth. "Just stay here. I'll be back."

Mother Tiffany hurries out of the temple. As the door slams behind her, Father John mumbles with miraculous clarity: "'Those who neither vote for sin nor for Mother and Father, shall elect sin.'"

†

Poopé Hal takes the stage with dung beetle farm in tow behind him. He keeps praying that he'll win the election so he won't have to move back into tract housing like just another urban slave. I remind him that after-hours clubs were sad until I brought the neon. He calms a little, but in the back of his mind, he thinks: *please* please *don't let her be pregnant!*

"I have been commanded," Poopé Hal begins, "by Mother and Father, in conjunction with our Liege's extended family, to warn you of the evil lying in wait on Election Day, and to direct you to—*a miracle!*"

The neon glow of "Hell, You Better Believe" shimmers in Father John's glossy eyes. Vaguely, he recalls the use of candles in worship during ancient times, before, in protest, the first Father lit himself on fire with the menorah and burned for fourteen days and nights, leading to the first cremation and the invention of the holy light, neon. Giggling, Father John finishes another bottle.

The congregation stares eagerly at the stage. After a moment they become anxious. Another moment passes, and their waiting grows loud with idle blinking and annoyed texting complaining about how long miracles take these days. Confusion begins to sprout from the ripe gardens of their minds, and they start thinking that maybe the Poopé is playing a practical joke on them… or maybe they're on one of those hidden camera shows… or maybe he's just testing their patience and their faith… or maybe he's just a *nut-job*, a quack! Growing impatient, they begin to doubt the Poopé's sanity, and, before long, they begin to doubt *Me!* I feel their doubt spiral through Me like vacuous tornadoes. Miracles take time, though, and considerable effort. When you make a birthday cake you don't just burst open a wrapper and—*poof!*—there it is. There are no Miracle convenience stores. There are ingredients that have to be mixed, in specific orders, baking times, etcetera. The parting of vast bodies of water, an afternoon wine drunk for a Woodstock-sized crowd, massive swarms of bugs—these things take effort!

The clamor of a profound insurrection of disbelief engulfs the crowd. Poopé Hal worries, but displays a stubborn unwillingness to admit defeat: "Have patience, members, and you will surely behold the *wonder* of *wonders*."

The doors to the temple burst open. The congregation gasps. The disciples shriek. Poopé Hal raises his arms theatrically as if *that* was the promised miracle.

It is Mother Tiffany dragging an elderly woman hooked to an IV pole behind her. "This man is a charlatan, a lunatic, a *Looky Lue!* He's been claiming to receive *messages* from Mother and Father—but it's a sham, and I can prove it. He said I was going to snort my grandma's ashes tonight, but *this* is my grandma!"

"I sure am. Where are we, Oprah?" Grandma says.

"Alzheimer's—she *is* my grandma. As the Word says, 'An array of years often dazzles the mind.'"

The "Word" she is referring to is *Cosmo,* June issue.

"She's r-right, y'all," Bobby says as he stands up, his voice squealing like a rat with its tail stuck in a trap. "Poopé Hal said I t-t-touched Suzy's boobs on my, on my, m-my—"

"He's nervous, everyone," Bobby's mom says, patting his back. "Just give him a minute. Bobby, remember what your speech therapist says, about forming your mouth around your words. And breathe. No one was ever reincarnated as a dung beetle for breathing."

"I'm not nervous, ma! Let me handle this for once"— Bobby takes a deep breath and practices silently forming his mouth around his words—"Poopé Hal said I touched

Suzy's… well, you know… on my *fourteenth* birthday, when it was really my *fifteenth!*"

Bobby's mom slumps down into her seat, shakes her head, and looks at the dung beetle farm, dejectedly. In the back row, now eighteen, Suzy frowns, lifts her phone above her head, and snaps a selfie. #SpinTheBottleFails

"*And*," Mother Tiffany says, motioning toward Father John, who is soaked in wine and smells like a peasant's feet after they've spent an afternoon stomping grapes.

"Father John—*testify!*" Bobby pleads.

After an elbow jab from the lady sitting next to him, Father John realizes he's supposed to say something. He stands, wobbles, falls onto his rear, stands again, and, swaying, announces: "Da poopy says dat he waz toed by, ya know—the one wit da boy and girl parts—dat I's been stealin' cash from the sin tax collection. But but but but erryjuan pays wit' *credit!*"

No one is impressed.

"*And…*" Mother Tiffany urges.

"Oh, oh oh oh oh oh—*Ohhhhh!* And he says tat I *fantasized* 'bout Mother Tiffany." He holds his gut and laughs inaudibly. "But *erryjuan* knows I'm—*gay!*"

Everyone shakes their heads in acknowledgment except for a baseball player in the back who is genuinely surprised. Mother Tiffany mutters to herself, "All the good ones are…"

"Is this all true, my lion?" Mary whines. "Tell me it's not true!"

"Mary, pipe down," Poopé Hal orders.

"How dare you! I don't care that we did—*it*. You lost my vote."

"Be quiet, Mary, before I tell everyone about your little *mishap* this past year on Celebration Day."

"What mishap?"

"You asked for it, Mary—you dropped the Celebration Day goat on the floor and fed it to Mother Tiffany and Father John without cleaning it off."

"I did not! I ate dinner at my mom's house. Mother Tiffany and Father John weren't even there."

My bad.

The crowd combusts with indignation. Assorted members shout out random questions about their intimate lives while others shoot curses at the Poopé's legitimacy. The disciples cower behind the Ark of the Toilette, holding each other and sobbing quietly. Working on the miracle, I wonder who it was that dropped the goat.

Enraged, Mary charges the stage, her body twisting and undulating like a surfacing whale. Stumbling, she falls headfirst into the Poopé's crotch, and he folds like a piece of foil. With Mary's weight knocking the air out of his lungs, Poopé Hal thinks: *maybe my therapist was right about the voices.* Members of the congregation rush the stage to help Mary, Poopé Hal or just to gawk, and the disciples break into an interpretive dance number in an effort to sooth tensions. The rest of the congregation begin to check their social media accounts as they file out of the temple.

"Stop—*Behold!* A miracle will come to pass," Poopé Hal promises, almost pleads.

Father John—a bottle of wine fastened to his hand—stumbles onto the stage. He quivers as consciousness forsakes him and he collapses onto the Ark of the Toilette, causing it to topple over, spilling the demons and their rancid booty.

"Run! For the love of everything holy—*run!*" Mother Tiffany screams.

The congregation does as ordered—screaming and scrambling and stumbling over each other, creating fire and tripping hazards up and down the aisles. Upon seeing the shattered glass of Hell and the giddy scurrying of its former inhabitants, Mary faints. The Poopé tries to pull himself out from beneath her, but Mary is beached upon his legs and he can't free himself. Only once in the annals of faith has there been such a prodigal hysteria, and that was when I'd left the masses to ponder their faith while I dictated The Good Trilogy to My grandson. Because of revising and My grandson's longwinded prose, My people were left worshiping a cow with mad cow disease for thirteen years. Not since then has the pestilence of faithlessness diseased My heart as it does now.

Bobby runs to the stage, brushing through the flock of stampeding nonbelievers. Falling to his knees, he tries to help Father John, but as Bobby takes Father John's face in his hands, he realizes that Father John is now nothing more than dung beetle fodder. Scanning the hysterical flight of the flock and then the dutiful farming of the dung beetles, Bobby feels a strange kinship to the beetles. *They're the most peaceful things I've ever seen,* he thinks.

Suddenly, Bobby feels a pinch of his ear. He looks up to see his mom, her eyes fierce with determination as she pulls him to his feet by his ear and drags him from the stage.

With My last ray of strength, I scrape My fingers through the temple and create a miracle.

"Lookie there!" Mother Tiffany's grandmother—who had stood blissfully still in amusement of the spectacle—crows. "I reckon it's a miracle!"

The word "miracle" spreads like an infection through the chaos, and the congregation stops and files back into the temple, firing up their social media accounts and directing the cameras on their phones at the stage.

On stage, the neon sign radiates so brightly it is almost blinding; it throbs like the heartbeat of creation.

The dung beetles suddenly pile atop each other and form a massive black huddle. A moment later in perfect unity they break the huddle and fan out across the stage, stopping in small groups along the way until they have settled in the shape of a crown. They stand up on their back legs, clap in harmony with their middle legs, and make lifting and swirling gestures with their top legs. The clapping makes a sound far exceeding what a natural dung beetle cheerleading troupe could ever hope to make, and its rhythmic pulsing through the temple quickly gets heads bobbing and feet tapping. The center beetles backflip and cartwheel onto each other, forming a pyramid, and then one beetle bursts from the center, flipping in the air at least three feet high! The beetle's flip concludes perfectly when it reaches the arms of its spotters below, who quickly roll the flyer to center stage. The heavy, spastic bass of techno music trumpets from unseen speakers, and, rocking his best Spirit Fingers, the flyer beetle asks in a deep voice: "Y'all ready for this?"

The crowd begins to sway with the beat, their eyes doubling, tripling, quadrupling, multiplying by unimaginable multitudes through the lenses of their cell phones. Videos are streamed and posted and tweeted, liked and shared and forwarded, across the vast formless cyberverse, reaching the masses of the world with such speed that all of creation is suddenly transformed into witnesses. The dung beetles launch into a gymnastics routine, dancing and flipping and twirling. They perform the Liberty, the Scorpion, the Show and Go, the Ground Up Full, the Bow and Arrow, the Superman, the Kick Basket Toss, the Paper Dolls, even the perilous X Our Triple stunt—all with flawless precision. It is a perfect routine, except for an overweight Back Spot whose smile wanes as she watches the Flyers flip in front of her.

Finally, the demons take flight and begin to sparkle like fireworks, forming "Vote Hal" in the air, before landing and dispersing back to their precious crap pellets. They roll their excremental relics across the stage and leave them at the Poopé's feet as if sacrificial offerings. Tucking their slimy heads to their bodies, they bow to him. I can feel the congregation's eyes on the demons as if on Me, and I can sense their awe. Quickly—*so quickly*—their reverence searches for a face, an embodiment, and their eyes cast upon Poopé Hal. Never before has faith in that temple radiated so incandescently; yet never before has shadow so poisoned Me.

"The demons have stopped, and they bow at Poopé Hal's feet and Mary's belly," Tiffany testifies, awe and wonder resounding in her voice. "Behold—*Mother*. Behold—*Father!*"

"Poopé Hal *is* Father. Mary *is* Mother," Bobby whispers.

Tiffany holds up her cell phone and kneels. "We've gone viral."

Mary awakes.

"Good morning, my butterfly," Poopé Hal says, directing her with a dramatic wave of the palm to the dung beetles and the congregation on their knees in worship before them. He has gone completely off script. "Will You take Your place at *My* side?"

"Mary is Mother. Hal is Father," the crowd chants in unison.

Poopé Hal likes the sound of it.

"Yes… *Oh, yes*… oh *God* yes!" Mary moans. "I will be the voice of Heaven."

The crowd averts their eyes from the blessed couple, the Parents of Man, Mother and Father. In the shattered glass behind the dung beetles and just seven feet away from

Hal and Mary, John's dead body lay, fuming the church with death and the bitter scent of wine. Next to him, the fading neon light flickers: "Hell, You Better Believe."

OCEANS

WITH HER FEET spread in stirrups and her knees pressed together, Mary's legs resemble the tentacles of a squid floating lifelessly along a deep sea current. Her face is blue, almost green—the way it looks when she has a stomachache.

Wading to her side—"Is everything all right?"

"I'm okay," she mutters, taking my hand and pressing it against her chest.

The hospital gown she is wearing is patterned with small green fish at regular intervals and is so loose that it reveals large seas of flesh, including the cold patch she is holding my hand against. Her dark eyes are hollow; a black wing of raven hair is cast down over the side of her face like a veil.

"Just leave it," she says the moment my free hand reaches to brush back the hair. "It's fine."

The ultrasound technician, a dark-skinned woman named Balianne, pulls the curtain closed. Moving with militaristic precision, she takes two steps to the counter, removes the lid from a jar of condoms, withdraws a condom in a black wrapper with gold lettering, and recloses the jar. With one step and one deft motion of hand, Balianne tears the wrapper of the condom open, steps on a lever that lifts the lid to the trashcan, and discards the wrapper. Two quick steps later, she is at the ultrasound machine. Swaying rhythmically, she picks up a plastic bottle of ultrasound gel and squeezes a dollop of it on the inside of the condom. She draws the ultrasound transducer out of the holster and begins to unroll the condom over the submarine-shaped probe.

"I expect you'll recognize how this feels," she says, neither coldly nor humorously. "Only this can't cause you any problems."

Once the condom is fully unrolled, she squeezes a precise line of gel over the top edge of the transducer. The image on the ultrasound machine brightens, and a second later the probe disappears beneath Mary's gown.

Even though the room is silent, it seems like the rippling images on the monitor are emitting vibrations too low for the human ear to hear but powerful enough you can feel them in your chest. Fixated on the monitor, it feels like we are traveling through the deepest depths of the ocean, the way science had imagined them to be before they had ever been glimpsed. Desolate, black—completely incapable of supporting life. An underwater wasteland threatening to suffocate any life that dare impregnate its belly. The ocean after science vanquished the Kraken and the sea serpent, and with ardor declared the giant squid a similar myth. The ocean when there were no glowing specters who could ignite the membranes in their angelic bodies and illuminate the darkness by just their presence—all-powerful life willing itself into existence before there was even will.

Mary has stopped looking at the barrenness on the monitor; she is now staring at her belly beneath the hospital gown, her eyes wet and bottomless. Her grip slackens; letting go, her hand slips down to her side, and her fingers coil like boiled lobster-tails.

As we sink down into the darkness of the room, as the weight of the ocean buries us, as our eyes bulge from their sockets, all there is left to do is stare up at the last ounces of water where light still plays, dancing with the waves. How shameful is it to feel relieved, even for a moment, that there is no Kraken to fear—that something doesn't exist, that it has, in fact, never lived, so you can continue on thinking and believing and acting the same way you always have? How heartbreakingly lifeless would the ocean be if we probed its depths today and found it as faceless as it had previously been imagined? How unimportant would our lives feel if we discovered the belly of creation was utterly empty?

FLYING

DAD HANDED ME the flashlight and climbed up into the rafters. Steadying the ladder, I did my best to aim the flashlight exactly where he had directed, but my imagination kept wandering back to a warm bed with fluffy pillows and a permanent snooze on the alarm clock. It was so early I could hear the Early Bird begging his mom for just five more minutes. I was doing my best to aim the flashlight, I really was, but my dad, being an old flashlight-pointing king, became irritated with my ineptitude and quickly descended the ladder. On the last rung, his foot slipped, and he tumbled backward, flailing his arms like they were wings and a few frantic flaps would send him airborne. Despite the waking slumber the rest of my body was buried in, my instincts fired on cue, and I caught him beneath the armpits.

"Thanks, Junior," he said, not especially gratefully. "Now if only we could teach you how to point a flashlight. I'll tell you what—why don't *you* find the paintball guns while *I* hold the ladder."

I nodded, suddenly irritated. There were two things my dad would say that grounded my spirits. The first was: "Why don't you…?" Well, I could think of a swarming hive of reasons I didn't want to climb the ladder, the most prominent of which was he just took a tumble I didn't care to repeat. The second thing he would say—and he would invariably say it with the smug, gloating tone of a wild robin taunting his caged cousin from a tree branch—was my name as he saw it—*Junior*. I always imagined he gleaned some sort of perverse pleasure by saying it, like the malicious glee that a vulture feels when it spots road-kill baking on the highway.

I followed orders and climbed the ladder. Dad held the flashlight's course steady, and I quickly found the paintball guns. As I came down, my mom opened the garage door and said, "Good morning, Captain Bill. Your breakfast is done."

And then, as inevitable as pigeons bombing your car immediately after you've washed it, she said to me: "I made you breakfast, too, *Junior*."

Having been a captain in the Air Force and a commercial airline pilot until he retired a year earlier, Dad's call sign as Captain Bill was firmly nested in the family syntax. And thus my designation as Junior was an unavoidable certainty, as dreary as storm clouds and high winds.

"I don't think we're going to have time for breakfast," Captain Bill said. "Junior and I need to get dressed and drive out to the field. This week paintball war, next week we're going *flying* in my new plane. Right, Junior?"

"Right," I groaned, contemplating how I could either lapse into a coma or flee to South America before the next weekend. Why exactly I had been stupid enough to make plans to spend two weekends in a row with my dad was beyond me.

"Well, I guess that just leaves more for me. I never thought I'd see the day when you two were spending every weekend together. Have fun, boys. But don't overdo it, Captain."

"I'll be fine," Dad said. "But why don't you pack me some bacon for the road?"

I changed into my army fatigues—which I had spray painted "Missed Me" on the back in neon pink—and waited for Dad to come downstairs. When he finally waddled downstairs, he was *definitely* ready for war. Outfitted in a button-down, pin-striped shirt, a fat-tongued purple tie, and a pair of flaming red Speedos, he looked like he was going for a job interview in a swimming pool. As usual, his silver chest hair sprayed out over his collar, making him resemble a peacock displaying his feathers, and his sandy brown hair lay like fuzzy wings over his ears. He was also drenched in Old Spice cologne; a tactic, I surmised, designed to act like tear gas.

"Are you ready to go?" Dad asked. Then I saw something I thought I'd never see: the old Air Force captain appeared happy—excited even. His brown eyes gleamed with the hypnotic glow of runway lights.

"Yes sir, Captain Bill," I said, saluting. "Private Bilbo is ready for action. But let me get you some camos first. I can't be seen with you looking like that."

I ran upstairs and got him a pair of camouflage pants. He sat down on the bottom stair, pulled the pants over his Speedos and slipped on his loafers, smiling contentedly. Finally, with considerable effort and an epic groan, he stood up. I decided to test just how magnanimous he was feeling, so I chirped, "Maybe we should take a wheelchair for you. You can be the mobile infantry."

"Sure thing, Junior," he said, huffing still. "And if we take a muzzle, maybe you could be the secret service."

A witty repartee? Was the jet stream at our backs or what? During the entirety of my adolescence, Dad responded to everything I said—from juvenile begging for worldly goods to hysterical pleas of salvation from the family Chihuahua who had had it out for me from day one—with the single phrase: "That's nice." And now suddenly there was good-natured banter between us; it was as if we had a true father-son relationship! For one brief moment, I looked forward to the next weekend when we were to go flying, but then...

"All right, *Junior*, let's get on the road."

Without another word, we got into the car and left.

†

We pulled onto the dirt road that led like a clogged artery through the heart of the paintball war zone. It wasn't a professional area; it was just five acres of isolated hills that were bearded with every sharp, sadistic form of vegetation ever spawned in the desert arena. The mountains surrounding us were painted with the pastel orange of California poppies, which were sure to match nicely with the sharp red and green paints we were going to dot the hills with. There were usually fourteen of us, give or take a man due to prior commitments, sickness, or short leashes pulled taught by overbearing girlfriend-types who never understood the importance of paintball wars. Today, though, we were all there, plus one.

We split up into teams, and Captain Bill just *happened* to be on the other side. The game was Capture the Flag, and our flag was at the bottom of a steep embankment on the southern edge of the field. Staying behind as a sniper to protect our sacred scarlet flag, I squirmed into some brush where I could spot approaching enemy troops. As the game began, the good guys surged forward. The gentle *tack tack* sound of paintball guns firing rattled the desert. After five minutes or so, the sight of an enemy soldier coming down the ridge toward our flag ignited my interest. It was Dad. He came plopping down the ravine like a duck waddling down a ridge into a pond. I had a clean shot from about thirty yards, but at that distance paintballs begin to lose velocity and seldom break on impact. When he was about ten yards away, he toddled through an opening between Joshua trees. Quickly, I capped off a few shots. *tack tack!* Dad fell to his knees and rolled behind one of the Joshua trees. Here was my chance, while he was blind and uncertain, to flank him. Confirmed kill number one of the day coming up, and it was *Captain Bill*.

I darted out of the brush to Dad's right. Most people are right-handed, including Dad, so they tend to look left when they are aiming. I took position behind a tumbleweed about fifteen yards behind him. Bullets may be able to pierce tumbleweeds, but to paintballs they're as good as armor. Just as I had thought, Dad was looking toward my previous position and to his left.

Dad moved forward, cautiously. I looped directly behind him and took aim. I had him dead in my sights, all I had to do was fire, but before I did, I wanted to announce myself as his slayer. I screeched, like a Red-tailed hawk soaring overhead: "Death to Captain Bill!"

Suddenly I heard the *tack tack* of enemy fire and paintballs popped like pigeon poop around me. I'd been flanked. I tried to cap off a few shots at Dad before I was a goner, but they were frantic and didn't come close. Feeling the sting of paintballs, I raised my hand solemnly, signaling my death. I'd broken two rules of engagement: Never get preoccupied with one soldier, and always keep your mouth shut when you're sniping. Apparently, Dad had been right about the muzzle.

A moment later, Dad captured the flag and began moving sluggishly toward their base. Jogging awkwardly, like a bird with a clipped wing trying to take flight, Dad clutched his left arm to his side and occasionally stopped to lean over and catch his breath. I knew he was out of shape, but I hadn't realized it was that bad.

Overhead, the smeared black halo of circling ravens shimmered in the glare of the sun. Although ravens were a common sight, it was still strange to see their perpetual funeral procession above us. Staring absently at them as I walked back to our base, I remembered the days in high school when seagulls would appear and swirl about with such a majestic freedom that the sight of them made your skin tingle as if you were facing into the ocean's breeze. Dad had told me once that seagulls were symbols of love. He was wrong, of course; it's the dove that is symbolic of love. But it occurred to me that the day Dad had talked about the seagulls was also the only day I ever remember him telling me he loved me. A stiff sadness blew away my thoughts about the seagulls as I recalled that I'd countered Dad's gesture by shrugging and refusing to look him in the eye. I had always felt like he loved flying more than he loved me, and I wasn't about to let any seagulls make me forget that feeling. A moment later, my attention returned to the ravens, which were moving off toward the east.

I reached base a few minutes later. "Base" was just a purple pole on the eastern edge of the field, toward the middle, just a few yards from where all our cars were parked. One of the rules of the game was that everyone got two lives, but to be resurrected you had to touch base. I touched base, resurrecting myself, and set back into the field.

I crisscrossed through the field, from front to back, retreating like a squirrel from firefight after firefight. In my own words, I was being a "Draft Dodger," but I had to kill Dad. I felt there was no better way to show him that I cared than with the bruising sting of paintballs. As I ran, I saw our flag flapping in the wind on the top of the hill where I'd last seen Dad. He had apparently handed it off or had been shot because now a guy that I worked with at Pizza Haven was carrying it. I yelled out, "Captain Wheelchair," and "Captain Cholesterol," over and over again, but to no reward. The game was nearing its climax. The bad guys had the flag nearly back to their base as a result of my selfish need to shoot Dad, but I didn't care. Today there were more important things than honor, pride, and victory.

Jogging back to the hill where I'd last seen him, I spotted Dad hiding facedown behind a cactus. It was a strange position to be in since he wasn't being fired upon, but it was strange for him to plan to wear Speedos to a paintball game, so I didn't think much of it. I looped around behind him and took position next to a cactus. After firing a few shots in his general direction to get his attention, I realized he hadn't moved. I fired again, but again he just lay there. My heart constricted. I rushed over to him, and as I did, I felt the splatter of paintballs bursting all around me. Voices echoed like distant sirens, asking if I was dead, but I didn't answer.

"Dad, are you all right?" I asked as I bent down next to him. It was then that I saw that he'd taken his mask off.

He was wheezing, and there was a scared, absent look in his eyes. Clutching his left arm to his body, Dad looked as if he'd been shot with a real bullet.

"Dad?" Fighting back terror for a moment, I tried to decide what to do. "Dad, can you get up?"

He shook his head. "My chest," he said, clawing at the hair splayed out over his collar. "Hard. To. Breathe."

"Okay. It's okay, Dad," I said, just as much to reassure myself as him. A gale of adrenaline swept through my veins, and I began to shake. We were alone in the desert miles from help. All I knew was that I needed to get him to the cars as fast as possible. "I'll pick you up."

As I stood with Dad in my arms, my back straining to hold his weight, I happened to glimpse the autumn sky. It was speckled with benign white clouds and was as blue as if the world were tucked beneath a robin's wing. Suddenly, inside—separate from the terror and confusion—an instinctual drive took over. It was as if invisible wings had begun to propel me forward at precisely the right moment like a mockingbird taking flight for the first time. With a strength outside of myself, I began to scramble back to where everyone had parked.

Then I heard Dad squeeze out my name: "*Junior.*"

"What, Dad? It's okay, Dad."

Racing up a steep embankment with two hundred yards still separating us from the parked cars, I could feel my legs, arms and shoulders boiling from fatigue. I looked down at Dad and saw a serene, majestic look in his eyes that was so unlike the absence and fear they had harbored moments earlier that it startled me. I was reminded of the seagulls again, and for the briefest moment, I could feel the ocean's breeze like breath on my cheek.

"We're flying… *Flying!*" Dad whispered, deliriously.

I didn't know what to say. Tears streaked down my face. Bouncing wildly around us, the sky seemed to be whisking us away to some preordained migration. I was running among the clouds, carrying Dad through them like a fleshly aircraft. Between the panic and exhaustion, I felt like I was in vertigo, spiraling through the sky with no idea which way was up or down. I looked at Dad again. He looked like he was floating away.

"Hang on, Dad. I—*I love you, Dad!*"

Suddenly, as if blown open by the sound of my words, Dad's arms went limp and fell to his sides. "We're flying, Billy…" he murmured, wistfully, one final time. Then William really was just *my* name.

ABOUT THE AUTHOR

"Some people run from their demons; others sit down and have cocktails with theirs."

William R. Hincy is a man who does and writes about the latter. Having become a writer after deciding it was the only sensible thing for a problem drinker to do, Hincy aspires to connect with readers on an emotional level while disrupting the precepts that great writing is inaccessible and there is only a market for stock plots, reboots and generic formulas. Widely published, Hincy's work is driven by characters who are both protagonist and antagonist, and who no longer create messes but have the mess. He now lives outside of Los Angeles with his wife and kids, having found solace in the notion that the only things sacred are self and spiced rum.

William R. Hincy's work has been featured by many of America's finest literary publishers, including Short Story America, Watershed, the Avalon Literary Review, Ellipsis, Oracle, Passages North, and Black Mountain Press.

Printed in Great
Britain
by Amazon